INNER SPACE

Merlin Fraser

Dolman Scott

Copyright 2006 by Merlin Fraser ©
www.Merlin-Fraser.com

This edition published by Dolman Scott
www.dolmanscott.co.uk

Cover Design by Bobby Rebholz. ©
www.freewebs.com/agediting1

All rights reserved. No part of this publication may be reproduced, stored in a retrieval system, or any form or by any means, electronic, mechanical, photocopying, recording or otherwise, without the prior permission of the publisher.

Printed for Dolman Scott in the UK

ISBN: 978-1-905553-19-8

Chapter 1

What a complete and utter waste of bloody time. These were the thoughts of Detective Inspector Nick Burton as he returned to his home patch after a fruitless trip to Wales.

He was trying to imagine if there had been an alternative reason for his boss to want him out of the office and out of town. He didn't think there were any secrets between them. After all they were a good team, as well as good friends, so why the silly subterfuge?

However, jammed in the window seat of an over crowded train carriage sitting next to a man of very ample girth, whose breath smelled of stale beer and onions, is not ideal to conducive thought. Opposite him across the dividing table sat the man's wife, a woman of equal size who fidgeted constantly and managed to kick him every time she moved, with a sickly grin and, "sorry dear," every time it happened.

As a distraction he tried looking out of the grimy rain streaked window, but with the gathering gloom outside and the bright lights inside, all he could see was his own miserable reflection. He grimaced at the sight of the life battered face looking back at him. It appeared older than his forty-five years. Once upon a time, it had been a handsome face, sitting on top of a well built body. However in those far off days he had had a relatively carefree, easy going attitude to life and he enjoyed the challenges life threw his way.

Twenty odd years a policeman had changed all that, carefree became careworn, easy going had become embittered. The all new politically correct police force and a legal system that cared more for the rights of the criminal than their victims had taken its toll. Add to that a broken childless marriage, a receding hairline, an expanding waistline and the promise of a stomach ulcer and you had his life in a nutshell.

He dragged his thoughts back towards the half assed reason as to why he was even on this train in the first place. His boss, Chief Superintendent Daniel Davies, or Dapper Dan as he was more commonly called, had sent him on this fool's errand to review evidence held at another police station. Evidence that, as far as he could see, was completely irrelevant to anything they were currently working on. He was doubly annoyed that given his well known aversion to travel that Dapper would send him on a job that could so easily have been handled by a first year constable.

Courtesy of his recent travelling companions and the time wasted exercise he was still fuming two hours later in the darkness of late evening as he walked towards his own police station.

As he pushed the front door open if he was expecting a sea of calm efficiency, which was the norm around here, he was in for a shock. The place was in uproar and most of the noise was coming from his colleagues.

There, milling in front of him, was a weird mixture of uniform and plain clothed policemen. The two different day watches were strangely intermingled; all seemed to be talking at once.

He pushed his way through the crowd to the front desk and the uniformed sergeant that stood there. As he approached he could see the sergeant was not a happy man. His facial expression seemed to darken even further when he saw Nick coming.

He asked, "Tom, you mind telling me what the hell is...."

The rest of the question died on his lips as the sergeant spoke almost in a whisper, "They've arrested Dapper."

Nick's jaw dropped. "What? Arrested... arrested Dan... what the hell for?"

"Murder," was the reply.

Nick shook his head. "No way, that's ridiculous, Dan arrested for murder, this is some sort of sick joke. Let me through, I want to see him."

The sergeant stood firm his hand on the folding lid of the counter; he replied as calmly as he could, "Look I know how you feel...but I can't let you in Nick."

"The hell you say," Nick replied. "The head of CID arrested for murder and the whole station standing out here with their collective thumb up their backsides."

Now the desk sergeant was getting angry, "look around you sonny Jim, we're all here because we've been thrown out. Internal Affairs is all over this station your office is off limits to everybody, especially you by express orders."

"Who's bloody orders?" Nick demanded.

"Mine actually."

Nick spun around so fast his vision blurred and a mild wave of nausea hit him. He put a hand on the counter to steady himself as he looked into the cold blue eyes of Superintendent Margaret Joy recently promoted and transferred to Internal Affairs. A more misnamed person would be hard to find, sm–all in stature she was as hard as nails and hated throughout the force for her fast tracked promotion through the ranks. Mostly, if rumours were to be believed, at the expense of her more experienced colleagues whose backs she had stabbed, robbing them of their successes. The over zealous pursuit of her new job put her at odds with practically every officer in the force and it seemed that in her opinion everybody was guilty until they proved otherwise. Her offhand way of dealing with her job had turned officer against officer and friend against friend.

"Of course," Nick spat the words at her. "I should have recognised your unmistakable handiwork a mile off. The ring of steel, jack boots tip toeing around, the sickly smell of burning flesh….."

Superintendent Joy just stood there a slow smile growing at the corners of her mouth but the smile didn't reach her eyes. "Careful, Inspector! Insubordination to a senior officer comes under my remit as well. Besides we need to talk."

"Talk?" Nick said surprised at his own calmness. "Just what the hell do you suppose we have to talk about? If you want to talk to me you'll have to trump up some charge and arrest me and even then I won't speak to you unless there is a lawyer present."

Her smile widened. "You're over wrought and upset, I can understand that. It can wait until the morning. In the meantime you're suspended from duty pending further enquires."

The colour was starting to rise in Nick's face. Their conversation was starting to draw the attention of the whole room. "Suspended? What possible grounds could you come up with to suspend me?"

"I would have thought that was obvious, wouldn't you? Your long association with the accused for a start, everyone knows how close you are. For all I know you might be an accessory to the murder and until I can establish the facts…."

Nick took a step towards her then checked himself. "My God! You can thank your lucky stars you're a woman because I wouldn't take crap like that from a man. You have no grounds to suspend me, I'm not some wet behind the ears constable that you can ride roughshod over. But if you want to pursue the matter we'll go to the Chief Constable right now."

The room was now still and silent Superintendent Joy realised she had gone too far and it was time to back away. "Have it your way, for now, but be warned I am your superior officer and I will not tolerate another such public outburst."

And before Nick could say anything else she turned on her heel and marched from the room.

Nick was trembling with anger. "That bloody woman who the hell does she think she is?" He pushed his way back to the counter and the desk sergeant. "Who's in charge upstairs? Tell them I'm here and I want to see Dan."

The sergeant smiled at him. Not many stood their ground before Superintendent Joy and it had been amusing to watch. "Dan's not here, he wasn't arrested here and we don't know where they've got him. The first we knew there was anything wrong was when 'Joy to the World' walked in with her goon squad and started to chuck their weight around."

"That's it, I'm out of here! If anybody needs me, I'll be at headquarters," and with that Nick stormed out into the street.

The cold night air hit him immediately, and brought him down to earth with a bump. As he walked through the cold wet streets his thoughts raced, what the hell is going on? Dapper Dan arrested for murder! He shook his head… No, impossible, some huge misunderstanding, it has got to be, there is no conceivable way that Dan would take someone else's life.

Who the hell is he supposed to have killed anyway? No one had told him that, mind you he hadn't asked. His mind turned to all the cases they were currently working on. He could think of several lowlife villains currently under investigation that would make the world a better and safer place if they were no longer among the living. But shit floats; sink one turd and another one just pops up to take its place.

The only thing that he could think of was that in some extreme case Dan must have been provoked or somehow caught so completely off guard that he overreacted. But one question kept nagging at him, why had Dan sent him out of town on such a stupid waste of time? Why today? Were the two connected? Nothing made any sense.

The night air had cooled his anger and cleared his head. He still had not a clue what was going on but he was determined to find out and before the night was much older. He hailed a passing taxi and headed for the centre of town and police headquarters.

As he entered the building he had to show his ID card to the constable on duty and then he had to sign in before he could see anyone. He had already passed at least six people before he saw anyone he recognised or knew him from Adam. He made his way to the duty Inspector's office and knocked on the door, only opening it when a polite female voice called out "enter."

He recognised her at once: Sandra Goodwood, quite a few years younger than him but they had worked on a couple of cases together when she was in CID. "Is the Chief in?" he asked, already knowing the answer.

She looked up from the papers on her desk peering over the top of her glasses and said, "Don't be daft, he's off to some wingding or other, left hours ago… in fact I think all the seniors are attending. Anything I can do?"

Nick went in and closed the door. "You've heard about Dapper, I suppose?"

Taking her glasses off she smiled, "Nick, I'm so sorry, I don't know what to say…"

"You could tell me it's not true, you could tell me where they're holding him."

"Don't you know? Dan's been charged with murder."

"You mean arrested?"

Rising from behind her desk she shook her head as she came towards him. "No, I mean charged. He was standing over the body in the hospital when they arrested him. He's confessed… signed a statement and everything."

The colour drained from Nick's face and he slumped into a chair. "I don't understand…Dan would never…it doesn't make any sense. Who the hell did he kill? Where is he… is he here… can I see him?"

Sandra was standing over him her hand on his shoulder. "I think you need to go home. Yes, he's here but they won't let anybody see him, especially you of all people.

Come back in the morning when the seniors are around. They'll be able to get you in to see him."

"Is he alright? Does he need anything? A... a lawyer, has he seen a lawyer?"

"He's fine, as far as I know. And no, there's been no lawyer, he hasn't asked for one, says there's no need."

Nick sat there white as a ghost, he didn't stand up... he didn't think he could. Sandra was on the verge of offering him a stiff drink when she remembered he didn't drink any more, or couldn't, to be more precise.

The room fell silent. All of a sudden Nick felt tired and sick. Shakily, he rose to his feet, holding the back of the chair for support.

Sandra said, "Let me get the duty car to take you home! Get some rest, start again in the morning. Honestly, there's nothing you can do tonight."

Her words were barely penetrating his brain. It sounded as if his hands were over his ears; he heard the buzz of a phone and he felt her arm gently supporting him. She led him towards a door that mysteriously looked both open and closed at the same time. The door moved and took on the shape of a big burly policeman. He heard muffled words, "Take him home... get him to bed... stay with him if necessary...."

The mist closed in and the voices stopped…..

The next morning Nick awoke with a start. He was lying face down on a bed but had little recollection as to whose bed it might be or where. His first thought was that it must still be the middle of the night, given the darkness of the room. He lay there, quite still, trying to gather his thoughts, listening for any telltale clue as to where he was. He had no memory of going home, in fact, as far as he could recall his last clear memory was talking to Sandra Goodwood... but exactly how long ago that had been he couldn't tell.

It was no good; he could hear nothing and his head ached. He needed to get up, he fumbled around in the dark until his hand struck something hard at the bedside. Gently he felt for the edge and moved his fingers over the surface until he touched something that felt like the base of a lamp. Running his fingers up the side he found the little switch just below the bulb itself. He pressed it and the room lit up before him.

It was his bedroom. He was lying on the wrong side of the bed, still in his street clothes with a loose blanket thrown over him. He thought of Sandra. Nah! Probably one of her men, the total lack of finesse as to his present state suggested the delicate touch of a beat bobby.

He swung his feet to the floor and went in search of his slippers. The bedside clock said 05: 36. A good strong cup of coffee was called for and as he waited for it to brew he threw off his clothes and wrapped himself in his dressing gown. He knew he must look a sight and in need of a bath and a shave, but he needed coffee first.

On his next journey towards his tiny kitchen he saw the little red winking light on the telephone that meant there was a message waiting. Even that was made to wait its turn. With a mug of steaming coffee in hand he wandered back to the phone, it shouldn't be that important. Anybody who needed him urgently had his mobile number. He pressed the rewind and waited for the machine to click and whir its way to the start.

"Nick! It's Dan. Listen, I don't know when you'll get this message but I imagine by now all hell has broken loose."

"Christ! That's an understatement and a half," Nick said aloud as the message continued.

"Most of what you have heard is probably true, and by now Internal Affairs will be all over the place. Whatever else you do, stay away from me. That's an order, probably the first I've ever given you, but I mean it! Stay right out of it or 'Joy to the World' will try and drag you in as well. What's done is done. I've no regrets and there's nothing you or anyone else can do to help me. Stay at home, go sick or take some leave, all will become clear if you stay at home."

The line went dead.

Second cup of coffee in hand Nick, played the message twice more before taking the little tape out of the machine and replacing it with a brand new one. Superintendent Joy's goons would undoubtedly search his flat, with or without his blessing, so there was no point leaving them any gifts. The fact that the message was there at all was testament that he had not been searched already. He thought, more fool you Margaret Joy, but there again you were always a piss poor detective. In her shoes he would have searched his place as soon as Dan had been arrested.

Standing under the power shower, his one real luxury, he let the hot water knock the ache out of his shoulders while his brain tried to make sense of what was going on.

His shock and the denial were over; it was true, and his friend and mentor these past seven years was indeed guilty of murder. But whom had he murdered and, more importantly, why? He had to know, even if it meant facing Dan and asking him.

Washed, shaven and in clean clothes he felt a lot better than he did last night. He phoned the station and talked to the duty sergeant, who informed him that the goon squad was still there. Apparently, they had spent the night packing everything up: computers, files, even the wastepaper baskets from the CID office. They had carted it all away in a hired white van. Good luck to them, thought Nick. The sergeant ended with, "Superintendent Joy left a message that she wants to see you here at ten o'clock."

Nick replied with a smile. "If she asks, you haven't seen or talked to me and I don't seem to be answering my mobile. If I don't have an office to work in I might as well take the day off."

"No problem sir," was the reply. "Anyway, I'll be off duty long before she even gets here."

Nick heard the line go dead and he listened an extra few seconds just in case there were any telltale clicks before he also hung up.

Decisions, decisions, thought Nick. Bowl of cornflakes or a bacon sarnie at the local greasy spoon on his way to headquarters? He stared into the small fridge, not enough milk for cornflakes. Ah well! Such is life.

It had just turned nine when he entered the headquarters building. A casual glance through a side window told him that none of the senior officers had made it in yet.

Obviously a good night was had by all, he thought. Although how they could just go out on a free binge with one of their own languishing in a cell downstairs was beyond him. Not something you need to dwell upon, Nick me boy, he thought to himself, the chances of you hitting those dizzy heights are a million to one. Then another thought chilled his brain. He knew one person who was clawing her way up the greasy pole and he shivered at the prospect.

The duty custody sergeant popped his mug of tea under the counter as he saw Nick approaching. "I've come to see Chief Superintendent Davies," he said as calmly as he could.

The man looked down at his desk and picked up a clipboard. "You're not on me list of people who's allowed to see him. Besides I don't think you're even allowed in here, are you, sir?"

"Look sergeant, what harm can it do? He's already confessed and been charged, so where's the problem? I only want to see if there's anything he needs, a change of clothes, a toothbrush or something."

"Five minutes is all you got and you have to talk to him from the passage, no going in there, and if anybody comes you pulled rank on me, alright?"

"Fair enough," Nick replied and followed the man to the cells where with a big bunch of keys he opened one of the doors and then moved a respectful distance away.

The sight that greeted Nick did little to improve his darkening mood. There, hunched on the hard narrow cot, was his friend looking tired, drawn and a little used.

Everybody knew him as Dapper Dan Davies, a good old fashioned copper, honest and well respected by all, even those he nicked. He was a tall and well built man from a fairly well to do family. His financial independence allowed him to indulge in his passion for being well groomed. He always wore immaculate tailor-made three piece suits over handmade shirts and coordinating ties. There was always a touch of gold about him from his cuff links to his father's old pocket watch with its chain strung across his waistcoat.

None of that was apparent from the tired unshaven wreck of a man sitting there before him. He had been stripped down to the essentials, the neck of his shirt gaped open and the double cuffs of his shirt hung open and dangling below his hands. The belt was missing from his trousers, as were the laces from his shoes. Rank had no privilege here. Nick felt the colour rising up his neck at the thought of Joy's goons manhandling this man out of his clothes and searching everything.

The old man looked up and it was clear from his expression he was not at all pleased to see his colleague. "Just what part of stay away from me didn't you understand, Inspector? God Almighty man, get away from me and stay away."

Nick looked crest fallen. In all their years together Dan had never pulled rank or even spoken to him in such a way. "I... I only came to see... if there was anything you wanted... needed..."

"No, no there isn't, just get away from here." The earlier sting was out of his voice now and he just sounded tired.

"Did those evil bastards keep you up all night? Did you have a lawyer with you? At least let me get you one of those....." The words were tumbling out in a torrent.

"Go home Nick, go home and stay there, is that clear? Everything you need to know is there. Now, if you have any respect left for me, get the hell out of here."

Nick was ready to start raving with more questions, but what would be the use? It was clear that his presence here was far from welcome. The fact that he didn't know why hurt him as much as if Dan had struck him in the face. He grabbed the door to the cell and slammed it shut with such force that the noises echoed around the hall.

"Sit there and rot if that's what you want!" he shouted as he marched passed the policeman with the keys.

There was nothing to be gained from staying here, it wasn't his case and as Superintendent Joy had so nicely pointed out he may even be involved. Back outside he wandered aimlessly, until the cry of a street news vendor caught his attention.

"Senior Policeman arrested for Murder! Read Allaboutit."

Nick almost ran to the newsstand, elbowing his way forward as he grabbed the paper from the man's hand. Quickly he handed over some money and was scanning the headlines as he walked away. He read over the sensational opening sentences looking for some hard facts, suddenly his hands tightened on the newspaper as he read:

Late yesterday afternoon detective Chief Superintendent Daniel Davies was arrested for the murder of a patient at the St. Anne's hospital. According to eyewitness reports he offered no resistance as staff restrained him while the police were called.

The murdered man was 34 year old Colin Murray, a long term patient of the hospital. Mr. Murray who, according to a senior member of the hospital staff, was completely paralysed from the neck down following a car accident fifteen years ago and would have been unable to fend off any attack. Also due to his paralysis his vocal cords were damaged and he would have been unable to call out for help. In this seemingly motiveless attack police and staff are completely baffled as to why

Chief Superintendent Davies would commit such a crime. This highly respected officer of local law enforcement is of course well known to this newspaper and we believe there must be a plausible explanation but it escapes our reasoning at this time. A police spokesperson said it was far too early to say anything...

Nick read on but there was nothing more he could learn, at least he now knew who if not why. He stuffed the newspaper in a waste bin and hailed a passing taxi.

"Where to mate?" the taxi driver asked.

Good question, he thought, where the hell am I going? "Just drive west for the moment."

As the vehicle moved away from the kerb he asked himself the question again, where to? There is no point going to the station and into the waiting clutches of Superintendent Joy. He still was not in the mood for another session with her or to run the risk of getting himself suspended. Can't go back to the flat, even Joy's goons would be waiting there by now... I need somewhere... somewhere I can think in peace and quiet, the library, yes! That'll do.

"Can you drop me at the central library, driver?"

"That's east that is, not west.... Still, it's your money!" There came an angry blast of a car horn from somewhere close behind them as the taxi driver hastily changed lanes, apparently without signalling.

Two hours later, stomach rumbling with hunger, he was no further forward. This is pathetic, he thought to himself. I have the biggest goddamn database of criminal information at my disposal and here I am sitting in a bloody library like a penny ante news hack.

He had been half heartedly trawling though microfiche records of fifteen year old newspapers.

Again, he had no idea what he was looking for; car accidents, even ones that leave their victim paralysed was hardly front page stuff. Let's face it... people get flattened every day, tragic but hardly news worthy.

Of course he had to admit to himself that he was not actually looking for anything in particular, he was just whiling away the time, or more precisely hiding. But hiding from what? He was not a criminal, he hadn't done anything wrong so why, against all logic was he ducking and diving around the city like a common villain? There was only one reason he could think of, joyless Superintendent Joy. Even here, other than his dislike for the woman, why avoid her? True, a small part of him realised that his disappearance would be a great sense of annoyance to her, and that gave him some pleasure. But why not face the cow? Get it over and done with, after all what could he tell her that would advance her case one step?

Then he smiled, what case? There had been a murder and the murderer had been apprehended and confessed, hardly crime of the century stuff. It would be almost laughable if Dan was not involved. They had got their man, so why was she still stomping through all their files? There again, maybe she wasn't. He hadn't checked in lately; perhaps it was time he did.

Once clear of the library he pulled his phone from his pocket and switched it on. It bleeped at him: there were seven messages. As he ran his eye over the tiny screen he saw that all the messages were from Superintendent Joy. So Joyless, he thought, you are still on the prowl are you...and he switched his mobile phone off again. She will just have to wait a little longer, there is no way I can face her on an empty stomach.

Lunch over, he caught a bus to the station and was just walking the last few hundred yards when a car screeched to halt just ahead of him. A large shaven headed man got out of the front passenger seat and faced him. Nick recognised him at once. "Christ," he said, "it's getting harder to tell real policemen from Mafia hit-men every day."

The man showed no recognition and even less humour. "The boss wants a word with you."

Nick thought he even sounds like a henchman. "I assume you are talking about Superintendent Joy? Your boss, not mine," replied Nick. "As you can see I am on my way to the station right now."

"The Super is not there. She's gone back to HQ. My orders are to pick you up and take you there."

Nick asked, "And you are?"

"DS Harvey."

Nick looked at his watch. It was nearly half past two. "Well, DS Harvey do you have a warrant for my arrest?'

"No, I was just told to go and get you."

"Shouldn't that be told to go and get you, sir? OK sergeant, you've seen me, you've passed your leaders message on. Now run along back to Mama and tell her that I have some urgent business to take care of and I will come and see her in her office at four o' clock, alright?"

"Sir!" The word was almost spat out. "My orders are…."

"Were you ever in the military, sergeant?"

"Yes Sir!"

"Well then, you should know by now to always obey the last order. And my orders to you are more recent now… bugger off….."

The man took a step forward but Nick stood firm. "One more step and I'll drop you where you stand." His voice was ice cold and the expression on his face said he meant it. DS Harvey turned on his heel and got back in the car which sped off tyres screeching leaving the acrid smell of burnt rubber in its wake.

That was stupid, Nick admitted to himself. Why antagonise the woman further? But he had resented her arrogance at sending one of her bigger goons to fetch him. Better be on time for their four o'clock appointment, he thought, or next time they may just have a warrant.

He pushed his way in through the station door. A constable at the desk looked up and buzzed him through the door. He ran quickly up the stairs to the CID offices, stopping sharply with his mouth open. There in front of him was a sea of empty desks with drawers hanging open. Wires dangled from torn out computers, leaving dust rings as evidence as to where they had been. Chairs were overturned and paper was strewn everywhere. Two of his junior colleagues were over in a far corner nursing plastic cups of coffee. "Looks more like a crime scene than a CID office."

DC Mary Riley was the first to speak. "It is a crime scene, sir. They've taken everything, even our personal effects."

"What about interviews?" Nick asked.

"They finished about an hour ago, we were the last two," this time it was the young man, DS Dave Martin, who spoke.

"So what did they want to know?"

"Just a fishing trip if you ask me sir. They just seemed to be going through the motions. I mean, what the hell do we know? They kept asking about some guy called Colin Murray and who was working on the case."

"What case?" Nick asked.

Mary chimed in, "Precisely, no one had even heard of a Colin Murray until they started talking about him." She looked around at the shattered office. "You can see they believed us."

"So," enquired Dave, "do you know who the mysterious Colin Murray is, sir?"

"Colin Murray is, or rather was, the man murdered yesterday by Chief Superintendent Davies," Nick responded in an almost casual manner.

Mary said, "We'd heard he been arrested but none of us could believe it. Not our boss, surely? It just can't be true, can it sir? "

Nick replied most soberly. "It can and is true. I heard it straight from the man himself this morning."

"But why?"

Nick smiled. "That… he didn't tell me so I know as much about it as any of you. Anyway, round up the troops for the morning. Get this place cleaned up and I'll see about getting our stuff back."

Four o'clock on the dot he knocked firmly on Superintendent Joy's office door and waited for the command, 'Enter!'

As he walked into the office he imagined he could feel the cold of her stare as she watched him cross the room. There was no preamble or formal niceties, no welcome of any sort just a blurted command. "Have a seat, Inspector."

Nick did as he was told, keeping his facial expression as neutral as possible. Without further ado Superintendent Joy got straight down to business. "I expected to see you this morning at ten o'clock. Didn't you get my messages?"

"No, Ma'am," he replied, "I didn't feel too well so I took a day's leave."

"Not sick enough to stay at home, or so I was informed."

"I wasn't sick, just not up to par. I thought fresh air might be more beneficial than just lying around the flat."

She pulled a blue folder forwards her and opened it. "This case you and Davies were working on…"

"Which case is that? We had at least four going on up until yesterday."

"The one involving Colin Murray," she replied, holding the file so that Nick couldn't see the contents.

Good try, thought Nick. "That's not a name I'm familiar with Ma'am. I don't recall the name being associated with any case we are, or ever have, worked on together."

"Do you actually expect me to believe you've never heard the name Colin Murray before this moment?"

Nick thought: now she was getting flustered, not only a lousy detective but a lousy interrogator as well. "That's not what I said. I said I don't associate the name with any ongoing case. I know the name from a report in this morning's newspaper saying that was the man murdered by Chief Superintendent Davies. Until then I had no idea who he was."

She changed tack. "Where were you all day yesterday?"

"Cardiff," Nick said with a sigh. "I was asked to go there and review the evidence they had on a local murder case to see if it matched anything we were working on, possible serial killer, that sort of thing."

"Who asked you to go?"

"Chief Superintendent Davies. It was a complete waste of time as it turned out."

"So do you think you were sent out of the way to prevent you from being implicated in yesterday's murder?"

My God, he thought. That was the first sensible question she has managed to ask. "The thought had crossed my mind, yes. It certainly makes more sense that way."

There was silence as the two of them looked at each other across her desk. Neither wanted to be the first to break eye contact, Nick blinked.

"Listen Ma'm, can I say something?"

"Be my guest, if it's relevant."

"I am in the dark as much as anyone as to why the Chief did what he did. As far as I'm aware it has absolutely nothing whatsoever to do with any case that CID is currently working on. In the seven years that I have known and worked with him there has never been any mention of a Colin Murray even as social acquaintance."

"Thank you Inspector, but that doesn't alter the fact that a murder has been committed and we need to know why."

"I too, would like to know the answer to that, and given time we probably will. However, the point I'm trying to make is that you have the contents of our entire department locked up in a white van somewhere and I need it back so we can get on with our job. Surely if your people have done any work at all you must have realised by now there is nothing in our system relating to this crime. You've got your man, he's confessed and been charged, therefore why is Internal Affairs wasting their time by investigating the entire staff of one police station?"

She stared coldly across the desk at him. "If we had had this conversation at ten this morning as I asked, perhaps your department might have been back at work by now."

For the first time during the meeting Nick smiled. "That would not have been possible Ma'am, perhaps if it had been a friend of yours arrested for murder you might understand. Besides I didn't find out who Colin Murray was until lunch time."

Margaret Joy closed the file she had been holding and put it with the others in a neat pile. "I'll arrange for your files and computers to be returned first thing in the morning. That'll be all for the moment."

As he stood to take his leave Nick thought, Christ she's a cold bitch even in defeat, but all he said was 'Ma'am!'

While he crossed the office towards the door she said, "It won't be made official until tomorrow but you'll be in charge of CID until a new Super is appointed. I believe a promotion to acting Chief Inspector goes with the job, congratulations."

If there was any warmth in the congratulatory statement he couldn't feel it but he added a "thank you Ma'am," as he opened the door and went into the passage beyond. Was it just his imagination or was it really warmer out here?

On his way back downstairs he mulled the meeting over in his mind. Christ, Burton, you are slow witted today! Joyless should never have told him about his promotion, albeit temporary, it was not her place to do so. It was so obvious that she just couldn't contain the fact that she knew something that he did not, a fact that she could only have picked up by talking to the top brass. Had she over stepped the mark by her raid on his station and been called to account? That would account for the relative softness of their meeting. She was just going through a face saving exercise by trying to put him on the spot. Kind of obvious now, her heart wasn't in it at all. No chance to use her brand new rubber truncheon, poor dear, he whispered with a grin.

Before he left the building Nick's thoughts turned to the prison cells in the basement. His first impulse was to go down and face Dan once more, tell him his fears about getting him involved were groundless. Get him in an interview room and find out what the hell was going on and what the two of them were going to do to get him out of it. Then with a touch of anger his next thought took him back to their previous encounter, what was Dan had said?

'Go home Nick, go home and stay there…,… now get the hell out of here.'

So with those words ringing in his mind Nick left the building and headed for home.

On his way back to his flat he stopped off at his local corner shop for some milk and the evening newspaper then popped across the road to his favourite Chinese takeaway. Now if there was something half assed decent to watch on the telly his evening was set. Tomorrow was another day not touched. He would start working out the why after a good night's sleep.

As he entered the front door, leading to his flat there was a small table set against the wall for mail and other messages. Nick put down his takeaway and other shopping and rifled his way through it. He whispered, 'Junk, bill, bill, junk, junk, offer of a free massage, junk, junk.' There was also a postcard from the Royal Mail saying that they had tried to deliver a package that needed a signature. He could collect it from the local sorting office, wherever the hell that is, he thought. He dropped the mail in with the rest of his shopping and stuffed the postcard in his coat pocket.

Chapter 2

In spite of all that had happened over the last couple of days, Nick slept soundly but awoke early. The bedroom was cold, meaning the central heating had not kicked in yet. Still there was little point just lying there, his mind was already racing thinking about yesterday, and wondering how to prioritise the day ahead now that he was actively head of his stations CID.

He was up, showered, dressed and sitting eating breakfast, when the phone rang. Instinctively he looked at his watch. It was still early, just past seven o'clock. He grabbed the handset. "Nick Burton."

A female voice responded. "Chief Inspector Burton, one moment sir. I have the Deputy Chief Constable for you."

He was just going to correct her about his rank then realised that, although no formal announcement had been made, she was right.

A deep gruff voice jolted him out of his thoughts. "Burton! Hardcastle here... wanted to catch you before you went to your station. Look, I want you to come to headquarters, something you need to know 'fore you go in, alright?"

"Sir! If it's about the promotion, I already know, Superintendent Joy....."

Hardcastle cut him short. "It's not about that. Just get here as soon as you can."

The line went dead.

Now what, he thought, phone still in his hand. DCC Hardcastle was always a bit abrupt in his manner but even so... Then like a penny hitting concrete. "Christ

Almighty!" he said aloud. It's seven o'clock in the morning, what had he said?

'*...just get here as soon as you can.*' What the hell was so important to get the DCC into the office at this time of the day?

Breakfast was now a memory as Nick pulled on his shoes and checked his jacket pockets for all the essentials. He grabbed his coat and headed for the door. Once out on the street he headed for the main road hoping to spot an empty taxi, his mind racing in several directions at once.

Luck was on his side, they seemed to spot each other at the same time. The taxi driver pulled into the kerb almost as fast as Nick's hand went up.

"Police Headquarters," he said and slumped back in the seat. A thousand thoughts came to him but none fitted the urgency. It had to be something to do with Dapper, but what?

He was none the wiser as he sat patiently outside the DCC's office. The pretty secretary, sitting behind her desk, was very deliberately avoiding any eye contact whatsoever. Suddenly the office door burst open and the mighty frame of the DCC stood in the gap. "Burton! Come in please." It was like a bark.

Just for a second Nick was reminded of an incident buried deep in his past, when a headmaster had used the same tone calling him into his study. Then, as now, he was frantically trying to think what he had done wrong to receive such a summons.

As he entered the room, the gruff voice ordered the door closed and he obliged as his eyes took in the room. They were not alone; the Chief Constable was also there. *What the hell is going on?* Two very senor officers in the building this early in the morning, it had to be about Dan. He had already watched the news on TV and there had not been any mention of World War three or another Great Train Robbery, so it had to be about his old boss. Well so be it, he thought, they are going to be mightily disappointed when they find out that I know as little as they do.

The Chief Constable rose from his chair as Nick came across the room. "Bad business Burton... damn bad business. You have my deepest sympathy, of course, but this is going to stink up the whole place you know."

Nick didn't know, and he looked at the DCC for support. The big man came up behind him and put his hand on his shoulder. "You don't know, do you? Nobody's told you..."

Nick felt his skin crawl. "Know what, sir?"

"Last night.... In his sleep, apparently... Chief Superintendent Davies died in the cells...."

The two men looked solemnly at Nick who looked as if he had been hit in the stomach. He could feel the DCC's strong hand supporting his elbow as he was steered towards a chair. He could hear vague mumbled words.... *"I know you two were close... Great shock and allthat... Can we get some tea in here?"*

"Burton! Burton! Are you alright? Here drink this, steady you up a bit, you're as white as a sheet man..."

"S-o-r-r-y sir, bit of a shock."

Nick took the proffered cup and saucer from the police sergeant. His hand shook and the cup rattled while he took a gulp. Tea... far too sweet... he shuddered but it seemed to do the trick, his head was clearing. "Sorry about that sir, it's just...."

"No need to apologise, man! Hit us all a bit hard, I can tell you... But you can see where it leaves us. The press is going to have a field day no matter what we tell them."

So that was it, Nick thought, afraid for their own backsides. There was a highly respected policeman with, until two days ago, an unblemished career lying dead in a cell downstairs. And all that worried them was what were they going to tell the media?

Through his thoughts Nick could hear Hardcastle's booming voice. "…they're bound to start speculating, was he murdered as part of some major cover up? Or did he commit suicide to avoid justice? Either way it'll look bad for us."

Nick felt the anger building in his chest. He wanted to explode and blow these two assholes across the room. Instead he said calmly; "I can't believe either is true, can you, sir?"

When the answer came it was the Chief Constable who spoke. "We'll have to get someone in from another division, make sure everything's done above board, out in the open, so to speak."

Nick turned and looked at him. "Sir, I was rather hoping you would let me handle this myself after all…."

"Absolutely not, completely out of the question! You're far too close, good God man, you were friends! He treated you like a son…. No, no, the press would…"

This time Nick let go. "Damn it, sir! Since when did the media take over running the police force? You know as well as I do we're on a no win situation with them, always grabbing the moral high ground. They'll damn us whatever we do. They call all the shots and we're stupid enough to let them."

Hardcastle moved in to intercept. "No one is saying the media run the police but these are changing times.

We all live in the spotlight of political correctness and all that."

Nick was going to respond but a pleading stare from Hardcastle said this was neither the time nor the place.

The Chief Constable continued, "the reason we asked you here was to try and throw some light onto this sorry mess. For instance, who is this Colin Murray and what was the relationship between him and Davies? Secondly, in your opinion was Davies the kind of man to take his own life?"

"Sir, I'm as much in the dark as anyone. Until yesterday I had never even heard the name Colin Murray. From what I've been able to find out he was the victim of a road traffic accident some fifteen years ago. There is no connection as far as I'm aware. Chief Superintendent Davies wasn't even the investigating officer. I was going to take a deeper look into the files this morning. And no, I don't think he was the kind of man to commit suicide. After all he didn't murder the guy and run away, he stayed to face the consequences of his actions. Plus I honestly believe there must be a perfectly valid explanation for all this if we just keep looking."

"Now do you see why we can't let you take charge of the investigation? Your opinion is already biased. The victim was a virtual vegetable; he was completely paralysed, taking his food through tubes without the ability to even speak. A more innocent victim would be hard to find, would you not agree Mr. Burton.?"

"Of course I agree sir, but there must be a logical reason for his action and I owe it him to find out what it is."

DCC Hardcastle was about to speak when the Chief Constable held up his hand and with a sigh he said, "very well Burton. I can't stop you, short of putting you on suspension, but I suspect even that wouldn't work."

Nick smiled, and thanked him.

"Don't thank me just yet I'm still not putting you in charge of the case. As I said that must be handled outside the division. All I'm saying is I won't forbid you from carrying out your own discrete enquires and I do mean discrete. Don't get in the way of the official enquiry, agreed."

"Sir!" Nick replied.

This time Hardcastle spoke. "Alright then, be off with you, CHIEF Inspector. I understand you have an office to put back together."

Nick rose to his feet and with a nod to both men replied, "Yes sir. Superintendent Joy is very thorough….not very effective but thorough."

"That's quite enough of that Burton," the DCC said as Nick made his way out of the room.

The Chief Constable spoke. "You were quite right to admonish him for speaking like that about a superior officer, but he's right about one thing. There's no way in hell that we can put her in charge of this one."

Hardcastle replied, "You're right of course, sir. Not one of our smarter moves putting her in charge of Internal Affairs. Bit like putting a bull in a china shop, no real benefit and a lot of bits to pick up afterwards, if you get my drift."

"Quite! Still we have to be seen playing these bloody silly political games, of gender and colour balance and all that. Personally I happen to think it's a damn fine idea, in principal, it's just there aren't enough suitable candidates and we end up promoting and using what we have. Damn shame really, but there it is."

"There's a vacancy for a Superintendent at Burton's station, if you're looking to move her, sir."

"Nice thought, but no, we'd lose Burton for a start, and when alls said and done it is a CID position and her record in that department wasn't too brilliant, as I recall."

"Good man, Burton," replied Hardcastle, "Pity we can't leave him in charge."

"Oh! I'll confirm his promotion soon enough, but it is a Superintendents position after all... still he'll do a fine job one man short and I'll not rush looking for a replacement for Davies."

Once Nick was back on the street he started walking. He knew he should get back to the station before the rumour mill reached the absurd but he needed time to collect his thoughts, again.

Christ! Dapper, what have you done now? Here I am trying to get my head around the fact that you have murdered someone, now this. His daughter! What about Jenny? I bet no one has told her about any of this. Where the hell is she these days? She married a couple of years ago just before her mother died, he was something to do with the Foreign office. Did they not move abroad, a consular job somewhere? Christ, I cannot even think of her married name! I really need to get back to the office; my bloody brain is addled by that tea. I need caffeine and a large dose.

By the time he reached the station he noticed there were already several people milling around outside. Hacks and their photographers, still locals by the look, no big tabloids yet, thank God. No TV either. He pushed his way past with one or two very curt "No Comments" and went inside.

No sooner was he through the door and the desk sergeant was the first to ask, "Is it true, sir? Is Dapper dead?"

Nick didn't answer, he just asked, "What's the word around here? Why is the press still here?"

The sergeant replied, "That's the trouble, it was the press what started it! They came in here as bold as brass and demanded to know if Chief Superintendent Davies had committed suicide while in custody. Bloody place has been in an uproar ever since."

"Right," said Nick, "put a constable on the desk, and get everybody else into the canteen. I'll be there in a minute."

With that he rushed up the stairs and into the CID office, which looked a little better than it did yesterday but still didn't look fully operational yet.

When they saw him the room was filled with everyone speaking at once, all asking the same questions. Nick held his hand up and said, "get down to the canteen, all of you, I'll be there in a minute."

There was a short silence followed by a wall of murmurs as they filed out of the room. Nick grabbed hold of DC Riley. "Mary, before you go down get into the files and find out what DCS Davies's daughters married name is and where I can get hold of her. Quick as you can, I'll see you in the canteen."

In spite of her pleading looks he was gone, out of the office and heading up another flight of stairs to the Station Commanders office. As he entered the annex the Commander's secretary looked up; "Chief Inspector, he's been looking for you," she rose from her desk and tapped on the door she had been guarding.

There was the faintest, "Come," from behind the door and she disappeared. A second later she was back.

"He'll see you now," and she stepped aside to let him in.

"Nick! For God's sake will someone tell me what the hell's going on? My CID office in tatters and that dreadful woman stomping all over the place chucking her weight around. My senior officers being arrested for murder my station under siege by the press and now rumours of suicide."

Nick smiled, "We're hardly under siege, sir. It's only the local hacks following up on the DCS's arrest."

"Well, let's get things nipped in the bud before we have the whole of Fleet Street on the doorstep. We're police officers! We're supposed to prevent crime not take part in it! Now tell me what's going on."

"I've taken the liberty of getting everyone into the canteen. I thought it would be easier if I explained it just once, don't you?"

Together they entered the canteen and silence fell instantly. Nick cleared his throat and started. "It's been quite a busy couple of days and there has been enough gossip, rumours and half truths floating about to start our own newspaper. Now, I've been given permission by the Station Commander to give you this short briefing to bring you all up to speed and tell you as much as I know. Which I might add isn't very much. As you are all aware Chief Superintendent Davies was arrested for the murder of one Colin Murray."

There were low murmurs around the room. Nick increased the volume of his speech.

"To end all unnecessary speculation I am here to tell you that the arrest was genuine and justified. DCS Davies admitted to and signed a confession of his guilt."

This time the voices were louder. Nick gave them a few seconds to air their disbelief before he went on.

"On an even more serious note, I also have to tell you that DCS Davies was found dead in his cell in the early hours of this morning apparently having died in his sleep."

Now there was uproar. Dapper Dan Davies was a popular man, a true gentleman detective respected by one and all both high and low. Nick raised his hand for silence and it took a while for the room to settle.

"Now I know what you're all thinking, but I must ask you all for your silent cooperation. As far as I know there is no suspicion of foul play, nor do I think it was suicide. It may be just pure unlucky coincidence but I must warn you all. This briefing is for your ears only, it is not, and I repeat, not a press statement. I will be very upset if I see or hear any of this repeated in the media. Is that clearly understood?"

Again the low murmurs filled the room.

"There will be a formal post mortem and we will await the outcome of that before starting any more rumours, is that clear? Now you all know as much as I do, so please let's return to our duties and get on with the solving of crime."

As the room slowly cleared the Station Commander came up to Nick, "Are you sure that's all you know, you're not just saying that?"

"Straight up, sir, I'm in the dark as much as the next man as to the whys and wherefores. But as God is my witness I will get to the truth if it takes me forever."

Once back in his office a cup of strong coffee in his hand Mary Riley came in with a neatly typed note. "Jenny Davies, or Mrs. Jonathan Smythe as she is now, lives in Oslo. Part of the British Consular office. Here's her phone number."

Nick thanked her and asked her to close the door on her way out.

For Nick the rest of the day was fairly routine: getting the office back into shape, catching up with the rest of his detective squad and getting up to speed on all outstanding cases. As the day drew to a close he went into the DCS's office, now his office he guessed. It was neat and tidy, much as it would be if Dapper was here himself. He was a very tidy man with only the bare necessities on his desk, but pride of place went to a framed picture of Dan's wife Patricia.

Nick sat in the big comfy swivel chair and took the picture in his hands. It was almost a formal portrait taken, as he remembered, on the night of their thirty-fifth wedding anniversary. Pat had been embarrassed by it but Dan had insisted on the formal pose bouquet in hand. She was a beautiful woman, in spite of her years and the advancing cancer that took her life just six months after this picture was taken. They had been a handsome couple. Seeing them at any formal gatherings, no one would have guessed this was just a policeman and his wife.

Nick pulled open the drawers, looking to remove any personal effects and was a little surprised to find nothing except the picture. His mind turned instantly and accusingly to Superintendent Joy and her bunch of goons, but why would they withhold personal effects? He wrote a note to himself to ask if everything had been returned to the office. He double underlined the word everything.

He supposed he should go over to Dapper's house and take a look around. The thought that it was not his investigation gave it a sense of urgency. Get there before whoever comes to take charge of the case. With that thought he pushed himself to his feet and said to the empty office. "There is no time like the present is there"'

On the way there he stopped off for a bite to eat and a quick scan of the local evening papers. He was pleased to see no more scary headlines and what news there was, was pushed deep to the inside pages. Hopefully, he thought, some other tragedy will befall some poor bugger and take the media's limited attention span away from Dapper Dan's story.

For a senior policeman Dan Davies had had a casual attitude to personal security. As Nick approached the garage he saw a small, hideous looking plastic gnome sitting forlorn on a rock. In an otherwise immaculate garden, it looked so totally out of place that it verged upon the ridiculous. But there, underneath that rock, Nick knew there was a key to the back door of the house. Twenty seconds later he was in the kitchen, door shut.

He went from room to room. All was neat and tidy, in fact too neat and too tidy, and he started to get an uneasy feeling in the pit of his stomach. He went back into the kitchen and snatched open the big double-door fridge freezer, the clean, shiny completely empty interior leered at him. He put his foot on the pedal bin and that too was clean and empty.

He went into the hallway to the telephone stand. He pressed the buttons on the answering machine and found nothing, no messages, just blank tape. He punched the redial button on the telephone and watched the digital numbers come up on the tiny screen. He recognised them at once: it was his own home phone number. Dapper's last phone call was the one on his own answering machine, telling him to stay away.

The bedrooms and bathrooms were the same, clean as a whistle. Not a scrap of paper, a dirty towel, nothing at all. Slowly he went through the house room by room. Even the desk Dan used as an office at home was devoid of anything that would offer a clue as to what was going on prior to the murder. In the end he had to conclude that this had been Dan's own doing. If Joy's goon squad had been here, which he doubted, then they too left empty handed.

Finally, almost as an afterthought, he went into the garage, all neat and tidy here too. Even the bloody car was clean, inside and out... nothing in the glove compartment or any of the other hundred or so nooks and crannies.

"Christ Dan, give me a clue! You owe me that at least."

Nick thumped the roof of the car in his frustration as he reached the conclusion that whatever had provoked his friend into committing murder it had been premeditated.

Dan knew exactly what he was going to do and how, he knew too that he was going to give himself up and that he would never return to this house. Was suicide part of the plan as well?

Nick let out an enormous sigh, whatever the answer is; it's not here. He looked around to make sure all the lights were off before locking the door and put the key in his pocket. As he did so his hand touched a piece of card. He pulled it out and stared at it, it was the postcard from the Royal Mail about a letter or parcel he must go and collect. He stuffed the card back in his pocket and went home.

Next morning, in the quiet of his office, Nick stared blankly at his computer screen. The trouble with not knowing what you are looking for is how the hell you know what it is… if you see it, he mused. He looked up in response to a tap on his door as Mary Riley stuck her head inside…"Coffee?"

"Oh yes please. By the way, what's the matter with you… nothing to do?"

"Plenty thanks all the same," she replied, "but you look as if you needed one of these," and she held up a big takeaway coffee with a plastic lid on it. It was one of those from the real coffee café round the corner from the station, not the cheap plastic rubbish out of the vending machine. "Need any help?"

"Inspiration is what I need."

"And coffee."

"And coffee," he replied, taking the lid off and letting the aroma hit him. "Thanks, I needed this."

"So," she said, "talk me through it, might help clear the mind a bit."

Nick pulled a pad towards him, took a satisfying swallow of the hot brew and started. "Who the hell is Colin Murray and what is the connection to DCS Davies? That's as far as I got."

Mary pulled out her little note book. "I haven't been able to find out very much but…..

Colin Arthur Murray, 34, has no known criminal record, not even motoring convictions or a parking ticket."

"Damn it Mary, he's been lying flat on his back in hospital for the past fifteen years hardly conducive to a life of crime."

"Hey! Who's telling this story? If you don't want my help or my coffee I can get out of here."

"Sorry, please continue."

"Colin Murray was injured in a hit and run accident just off the London Road east bound out of town at 11:30 on Friday the 20th July 1990. He was changing the rear offside wheel of his car when he was struck from behind by a 1987 dark blue Jaguar XJ6, being used as the getaway vehicle following the robbery of Martin's jewellery shop in the High Street twenty minutes previously. The vehicle was being pursued at high speed by police patrol vehicle 'Charlie Foxtrot'. Following the accident they were forced to abandon the chase, owing to Murray's body lying in the middle of the road. The officers called for backup. The Jaguar was found abandoned and burnt out three days later. It had been reported stolen two days prior to the robbery."

"OK, so where was DCS Davies at that time?"

"He was only a Chief Inspector in those days."

"Only a Chief Inspector," Nick looked at his young assistant, who blushed scarlet.

"I didn't mean..."

Nick laughed. "I'm teasing you, go on with your not very much but...."

"Chief Inspector Davies was on his way to hospital having received gunshot wounds in his attempted apprehension of the thieves leaving the jewellery shop.

Apparently one of the shop assistants triggered a silent alarm and by coincidence DCI Davies was part of an observation unit close by and went to the scene."

"Shot?' Nick said sitting bolt upright, "I never knew he had ever been shot."

"It's true sir, he was given a medal and a public reception, the works."

"So," said Nick, "that's the connection. DCI Davies was shot trying to prevent a robbery in progress and twenty minutes and God knows how far away from the crime scene Colin Murray was run over by the getaway car. So why would Daniel Davies, now a Chief Superintendent, suddenly take it into his head to murder Colin Murray some fifteen years after the fact? It doesn't make any sense at all, or have you got the answer to that one in your little black book as well?"

The shocked and pained expression on young Mary's face hit him like a slap.

"Mary, I'm sorry! That was a bloody stupid thing to say, please accept my apologies."

"That's alright sir. He was your friend, we all know that and this is a bit of a shock."

"Even so it's no excuse for bad manners and being rude. You've done an excellent job here, better than me." He stretched into his pocket. "Tell you what…how about some more of that coffee? No, better still, let's go there together and I'll buy us lunch."

On their way out of the station Nick paused at the front desk. "Sarg, any of your patrols go anywhere near the local postal sorting office? Can you get them to collect this for me," and he handed him the battered postcard.

The sergeant looked at it. "Says here it needs to be signed for…"

"Just tell them its vital evidence in a criminal case and threaten to do them in for obstructing justice, or something."

Lunch over, Nick sent Mary back to the office and went for a walk in the park. The more he thought about Dan Davies the more it dawned upon him that he really didn't know the man at all. Dan had treated him like a son. They had been a good working team with many solved cases and solid convictions to their credit. They called each other friend but when all was said and done, did he know who Dan Davies really was?

Sitting on a bench facing the duck pond he thought, let's face it; I have only known him seven years, hardly a lifetime. Now it was becoming blatantly apparent that the man had had a whole life that I knew nothing about. Why did it come as such a shock to learn that Dan had once been shot in the line of duty? But what was truly shocking was the sudden realisation that this terrific, gentle man, his boss, his mentor and yes, his friend was capable of premeditated cold blooded murder. And then apparently, just as coldly, commit suicide.

Then as his thoughts continued shock turned to anger in Nick's mind. OK friend, answer me this: why murder? Why go it alone? You bastard! I would have followed you to Hell and back, all you had to do was ask. Now I may never even know why.

Nick piled his clenched fist into the cold hard wooden seat of the bench. The sudden pain brought him back to reality. He felt ashamed at his anger but it did little to suppress the great loss he felt inside.

The late afternoon gloom was falling over the town as he returned to the station. As he came in, the desk officer passed him a small brown padded envelope. It was fairly fat and when he got it into his hand it felt like a video tape. Stuck to the outside of the envelope was a yellow sticky note, which read: *'If it's Porn... Me next!'*

Nick smiled and popped it into his coat pocket. After all it was sent to his home address and might have nothing whatsoever to do with the police, but somehow he doubted that.

A quick tour of the office, a look through the phone messages and a ten minute debriefing session with those in the office and he was off home. A shouted reminder to them that they knew where to find him if needed was tinged with enough threat that he would rather they didn't. The video in his pocket was burning a hole. Somehow he knew it was important and like a kid he couldn't wait to get home.

He was going to visit the local supermarket and pick up something half decent to eat but the thought of any further delay in finding out the video's content suggested otherwise. He made a decision as well as a promise to his stomach: an Indian takeaway tonight, something decent with a salad tomorrow night.

Everything set, TV on, video in place, Nick sat down with the remote control in hand and a tray of food and drink on his lap. He was ready to go but to where he had no idea. The envelope contained no clues as to the subject matter of the video. Even the label was typed on a laser printer and the post mark was smudged. He pressed the play button and waited.

The normal TV picture vanished to be replaced by black and white snow and the hiss of static. This continued for so long he was sorely tempted to press the fast forward button when suddenly a female voice asked, "Is this bloody thing working or what?"

Shortly thereafter a fuzzy picture of a ceiling came into view and wobbled around to the sound of the same female voice asking, "Why didn't you set it up properly beforehand, Pillock? The lecture is about to start... look he's coming."

The camera angle left the ceiling and panned down towards the ground. Then the backs of various heads came into view and vanished as the camera now looked over the top of them, to what Nick assumed was a stage with a blob on it. Slowly the image cleared and went through and then back into focus. Then a new voice, male this time, said, "There you are. Are you happy now?"

The reply was muffled but Nick still made out the word 'Pillock'.

Then from the man on the stage:

"Good evening, ladies and gentlemen. My name is Professor Harman-Jones and I thank you for coming out on this rather cold blustery evening. I trust you will find the subject matter enlightening and the views not too extreme."

Nick looked closely at the man. He was scholarly in appearance, above average height with a slight stoop, mid fifties. His face was almost obscured, surrounded as it was in a full shaggy grey beard topped off by a shock of grey hair. The thick framed glasses he wore gave his face an owlish look. However, given the almost immediate silence that fell upon the room he was certainly a well respected speaker. Without further ado the professor continued;

"As many of you who have attended these lectures before will no doubt remember, my opinions of the American space programmes and their NASA space agency in particular. For a small fraction of the money they waste on fruitless research I believe we here could advance many of mankind's exploration projects."

"Why are their efforts such a waste of time and money? Well ask yourself this other than round and round in circles, where exactly do they think they're going? They may eventually send manned missions to Mars but as for deep space it is a forlorn hope."

"Let us review the facts,"

... and, as if for effect, the large screen behind the professor came to life with what looked like a totally black image. It was only upon closer inspection that it revealed itself to be a picture of the dark heavens.

"Behind me is not a simple image taken by pointing a camera skywards at night, but one of the last pictures taken by a NASA probe. Voyager was launched some twenty-eight years ago in 1977. This picture was taken in 1990 as the probe was leaving our Solar system. This..."

And there was a loud, almost contemptuous, slap as the professor's pointer hit the screen.

"This insignificant tiny dot of light is our sun at a distance of some 4 billion miles. An impressive picture, I think you will agree, but one that took thirteen years to take."

"The universe... No! Let's be even more realistic, our own galaxy is so vast it has to be measured in light years. A term used to bring the enormous numbers involved down to a size we mortals can comprehend. Our galaxy is estimated to be 100,000 light years in diameter. To turn that into miles would require more zeros than this wall and our brain could handle and would indeed be a meaningless number."

"In their terms our sun's nearest neighbour is a mere four light years away. Put like that it sounds close enough. It took poor tiny little Voyager thirteen years to travel the four billion miles merely to get to the edge of our own star's system. The next nearest star to our own Sun is twenty-four trillion miles away. Travelling at the highest known velocity for a manmade object in space, you're looking at a journey of say twenty to twenty-five thousand years, give or take a thousand or so either way. And! If that's not enough bad news, there's nothing there when you arrive."

There was a ripple of laughter.

"As you know, I have little interest in science fiction, save for the great number of inventive ways they have for their heroes to cover great inter stellar distances in as short a time scale as possible. Let me see, there's the famous warp drive, jumping through hyper space, wormholes Star drive and I'm sure a dozen others. The one thing they all have in common is that they all recognise the need to travel at speeds vastly greater than the speed of light itself if they are ever to get anywhere. Mind you, while they are at it they had better develop those shield things they love to talk about. Because even at just the speed of light you will see very little of what is in front of you before it is actually behind you. Can you imagine the damage that even a grain of sand would do hitting you at that speed?"

"So, clearly, man is not destined to go exploring the galaxy any time soon. A fact our world leaders might take seriously into consideration at the next summit to discuss global warming and the ozone layer."

At this there was first a laugh, then applause.

"Are we alone in the galaxy or the universe? I for one seriously doubt it…if we are what a hell of a waste of space for just one miserable species. No, I believe the vastness of outer space is teaming with life."

"Will we ever meet? Probably not, for exactly the same reasons that plague us their inability to cross the great distances involved."

"Of course there may be a more divine or philosophical reason to explain the vastness of the universe; given the fact that the population of our own tiny planet has an inability to live peacefully together, it may be by design to prevent any interstellar cohabiting. I let you be the judge."

"In science fiction they look to space as the final frontier for man to explore, although I think we have established here tonight that it is unlikely to happen certainly any time soon."

"Unless that is, we first conquer Inner Space before returning our attention to Outer Space."

"When Einstein made his statement that nothing in the universe can exceed the speed of light, he was of course speaking of things that have mass. Quite recently there has been a lot of speculation that Einstein's theories may not be one hundred percent true for the behaviour of light itself. So for the purposes of tonight let us assume that the rules hold true for everything solid. Will man ever have the ability to transport matter via light, who knows? While such a device may hold great advantages over relatively short distances, say here on Earth but as means of inter stellar travel…? And here again they would still be constrained to the ultimate speed of light and the vast distances I mentioned before."

"However, there is one thing that can travel faster than even light itself."

As if his feelings were shared with the audience on the tape, Nick was holding his breath, scared that he might miss the next sentence.

"Thought!"

The single word hung in the air like the final note from a giant bell. It was almost an anticlimax. There was the sound of people moving in their seats, whether this was from relief or a release of tension, Nick didn't know. He wanted the professor to go on, to explain himself before he lost his audience.

"That's correct," the voice continued. *"A single human thought travels faster than anything in whole of the vast cosmos."*

The room was stirring. The murmurs were getting more audible. The man in the centre of the stage lifted his hand in the air.

"Now before you dismiss this as rubbish, let us just think about it for a moment."
"As an experiment try it now for yourself. Sit back in your seat and make yourself comfortable. Now close your eyes and relax. Think about your home or a favourite place, somewhere you remember being happy. Think of who you're with... a friend... a loved one..."

The voice was becoming almost hypnotic, a series of whispered commands. Nick could not resist joining in; he pushed back in his armchair and closed his eyes listening to the voice. At first there was nothing, just the darkness and the voice, and then there was light…. He could see….see people messing about down by a river. There was a girl… very pretty, sitting quietly off by herself, a boy nervously approaching from behind her. She looks up and around at him and smiles… then he is kneeling by her side holding her, looking at her as their lips touch, lightly at first then harder. He could taste the sweetness of her… smell the faint hint of lavender on her skin… Nick's eyes sprung open. His first real kiss, the sensation was so real, my God he thought, I can still smell her perfume….I….I was there. In the background the professor's quiet voice continued bringing his audience back to reality. Nicks' first thought was 'Wow! I don't know what you're selling my friend, but I'd buy some.'

With a loud clap of his hands professor Harman-Jones regained their attention.

"Now a brief show of hands, how many of you just took a little journey into the past?"

There were quite a few arms waved in front of the camera.

"Good! Now perhaps you may have an inkling of the point I am trying to make. The human brain is capable of far greater things than we at present can comprehend. For instance, would it surprise you to know that it is estimated that we can control only about ten percent of our brain power? Much of our brain function is automatic, controlled by our bodily needs. Only in certain key areas such as sport and academia do we stretch our brain capacity. But for the most part

we are content to live our lives comfortably controlled by our inbuilt computer system."

"There are many known examples of man's ability to achieve almost superhuman feats, using nothing more than brain power alone. Indeed there are many of us who believe that over the centuries man has lost many of the mind skills he once possessed and we have dedicated our lives to retrieving some of those lost skills."

Nick sat enthralled through the rest of the tape as the professor sited many examples of the lost art. He seemed to perform a couple of experiments that proved that man could move objects with just the power of his mind.

When it was all over he just sat there looking at the TV screen. OK! It had been fascinating, so what? But when he looked down at his lap, the food on the tray was largely untouched and stone cold. He had been scooped up and carried along, but to where? What was the point? Who had sent him the tape and more importantly why?

Nick sat there for ages mulling it over in his mind and getting nowhere. It was still uppermost in his thoughts as he finally got up and went to bed. But, even there lying in the dark his thoughts still raced. He closed his eyes and slowly he recalled that low whispering voice… *"a favourite place somewhere you remember being happy. Think of whom you're with… a friend or a loved one…"*

And once more he was there under the shade of a tree with the girl on the banks of that river thirty years ago.

Chapter 3

The following day last night's video experience faded fast in the cold hard light of morning. Nick thought that it had been interesting, no more than that. Enthralling, but it had little real significance to him or anything in his life.

The trials of day to day police work soon pushed the memory to the back of his mind, as the short holiday granted to the local villains caused by Superintendent Joy's disruption to the CID office came to an end. Back at work and now in charge, albeit temporary, Nick was soon in the thick of things. He presided over Morning Prayers, as the irreverent called their daily review meeting, setting the priorities for the day ahead. He listened to the moans about hours in the day, lack of resources and manpower, while acknowledging the fact that the criminal fraternity didn't seem to suffer from the same problems.

As the meeting broke up, DC Mary Riley held back as the others filed out. In her arms was a big fat parcel that bore all the tell tale signs of being old and forgotten. Wrapped in brown paper and tied with hairy string she dropped it onto his desk where the unmistakable smell of old paper and dust hit his nostrils. "You might find this of interest. It's an open file on the jewellery store robbery in July 1990."

Nick looked at her in shock. "Still open?"

She smiled back at him. "Forgotten more like. No one was ever caught or convicted of the robbery or the shooting. I'll help you go through it, if you like."

He smiled back. "Thanks, I'll bear that in mind, but for now let's just focus all our attention on the present bunch of 'ner-do-wells' on our patch. After all they're still hurting people."

That said Mary took her leave but Nick could not help wondering what kind of story lay hidden in that parcel and more importantly when would he get the time to look at it. For the time being he dropped it onto the floor at the side of his desk as the phone rang.

Nick snatched the phone from its cradle, as he spoke his name the familiar gruff voice of the Deputy Chief Constable cut him short. "Hardcastle here just thought you'd like to know the post-mortem on Davies is in. Not a lot of help though, cutting through the medico speak all it says is the chap died of natural causes. What do you think about that, me boy?"

"Not much, sir. As you said it doesn't help us one way or another. Mind you, I never thought for a moment that the Super would commit suicide, not his style."

There was no comment from the other end. "Just thought you'd like to know…"

"Yes sir, thank you sir," but the line was already dead. He looked once more to the file on the floor and said softly, "Damn it Dan! If you've taken the secrets to your grave I may never forgive you."

The phone rang again and pushed old cases and the memories of Dapper Dan clear out of his mind.

The weekend was upon him before he realised it. It had been an event-filled week that was for sure. Normally he wouldn't have gone into the station on a Saturday but today he did. He chatted to the uniformed sergeant about the previous night's activities, went through his messages and emails and then, cup of coffee in hand, he closed his office door and took up the parcel off the floor.

Once opened he separated the contents into heaps… there were typed reports, witness statements, reports and pictures taken from the close circuit TV cameras in the shop and press cuttings. There were two different coloured file covers. The buff ones seemed to cover the robbery itself and the blue ones covered the shooting incident. Nick resisted the urge to go straight to the blue folders. As much as he wanted to know about the gunning down of his old friend, it seemed that it was a simple case of being in the wrong place at the wrong time. So he turned his attention to the robbery itself.

The armed robbery took place on 20th July 1990 at 11:12, or at least that was when the silent alarm had been triggered. Slowly and meticulously he sifted and sorted his way through the files, making notes in a separate note book for his own use later. With a fresh cup of coffee in hand he reviewed his notes:

Prior to the robbery there were three staff and two customers in the shop. The shop manageress (a long term staff member). A salesman (also a long term employee) and a woman who worked part time. The part timer had only been employed a few weeks but it was she who had triggered the alarm.

The two others in the shop were a very well dressed old lady in a wheelchair assisted by a uniformed chauffeur. The blue Jaguar car used as a getaway vehicle apparently belonged to the old lady. **(WHERE WAS THE OTHER CAR ?)**

Two large men, wearing dark blue boiler suits with black Balaclava ski masks covering their faces, burst into the shop. Both were described as white males and one had blue eyes. Both men were armed, one with a single barrelled pump action sawn-off shotgun, the other with a hand gun.
(Later identified from the bullets recovered as a 9mm revolver).

The first man threatened the staff in an Irish accent, **(Probably false)** *while the second disabled most of the CCTV cameras. One camera remained functional throughout, but was useless for identification purposes due to being behind the main figures.*

The second man then held the old woman hostage, threatening her life if the staff did not cooperate. The first man threatened and then coerced the chauffeur into helping with bagging the proceeds from the robbery.

The main items of interest were a large packet of uncut diamonds stored in the safe.

Other items were the money in the shop safe and what could be quickly taken from the cash register. Next shop displays, mainly diamond rings and high quality watches.

When the alarm finally sounded the two men took the old woman and her chauffeur as hostages and made a run for it. The wheelchair was abandoned in the street as the hostages were manhandled into the car.

It was at this time someone shouted: "Armed Police! Stop and give yourselves up."

Two plain clothes policemen had arrived on the scene, having been alerted to the robbery by radio. They had been assisting the drug squad on observation duty at a house just off the high street **(neither was actually armed).**

The robber previously said to have blue eyes turned and fired two shots at close range. Both hit Chief Inspector Davies: one in the upper thigh and the second low in the abdominal region.

The car sped away at high speed. It was intercepted and pursued by police patrol vehicle 'Charlie Foxtrot.' On the way out of town the police car was forced to abandon the chase following the accident involving Colin Murray.

Based upon information from the crew of Charlie Foxtrot other patrol vehicles were redirected to intercept the Jaguar. Based upon the assumption that it was heading for the motorway and probably London. No further positive sighting of the vehicle were made.

The Jaguar was found abandoned and burnt out three days later, in a wood on the outskirts of a village having escaped detection by going cross country. The car had been reported stolen two days prior to the robbery. Follow up investigation proved that the owner was not a wheelchair bound lady nor was there a chauffeur. **(Surprise, surprise!)**

No one fitting the description of the lady or her chauffeur was ever reported abducted. No reports of anybody fitting the description being found abandoned, finally led the investigation team to conclude the couple maybe part of the gang.

Final conclusion was that the gang of robbers was probably five not two, to include one woman, **(possibly)** *and a getaway driver never actually seen.* **(Local boy?)**

All leads were followed up and failed.

The file remains open and was reviewed twice. Once in 1993 and again in 1995, when there was a marked similarity to other jewellery store robberies in other parts of the country where the M.O. had been matched.

No arrests were ever made in any of the three reported robberies.

Nick closed his note book and put it in his pocket. The fact that one of their own had been shot during the crime would have added extra momentum, but in spite of that fact no one was ever arrested for the crime. Nick could see no fault in the methods of their investigation. The trail had just gone cold. There was obviously a good brain behind these crimes, they were not greedy and they were not stupid.

The folders detailing the actual shooting itself, and the separate investigation gave him no more real information.

A lot of gory medical details complete with pictures. Forensic evidence of the type of gun, using pictures of the bullets or what was left of them. There was a lot of cross referencing to the robbery investigation, but sticking to the witnesses in the street of the actual shooting incident.

Nick imagined that given the sheer speed of the whole thing, the statements taken were remarkably detailed, which to him meant that they were more imagination than fact.

He tidied up the files and the rest of the paperwork, putting them back into the neat brown paper parcel, ready to go back to the archives. With an almighty sigh and a long stretch he concluded that his efforts had increased his knowledge but failed to put him one step closer to finding a logical conclusion to the present mystery. As far as he could see, Dan Davies and Colin Murray were both victims of the same criminal gang. Both just happened to be in the wrong place at the wrong time, so why would one end up killing the other? It just didn't make sense.

A few hours later, carrier bags of shopping in both hands, Nick pushed his way through the front door of the building containing his flat. There on the small table was some mail for him. Most of it looked like junk mail. He was temped to just leave it until a more convenient time but a large manila envelope intrigued him. Slightly irritated he was forced to put his shopping down to retrieve the post.

Once he reached his flat, he flicked through the mail. His first assumption that the vast majority of it was junk proved correct but the large envelope looked far more interesting. He tore it open to reveal what looked like police investigation folders. A thought sprang into his mind: now what? However as intrigued as he was he resisted the urge to sit down and devour the information.

He was cold and hungry, he had been shopping and had bought some real food, which he fully intended to cook and enjoy. Everything else would have to wait. But of course they did not have to wait for long. No sooner had he finished the washing up, coffee in hand he returned to the table with the two buff folders and sat down.

The first related to a bizarre accident involving a man hitting a train. Nick read the opening statement again, man hitting train, not the other way around, interesting start. It seems that the incident had all the hallmarks of someone jumping from a bridge into the path of an oncoming train.

However in this case the incident happened on a straight piece of track in open countryside without a bridge, or any other tall structure for that matter. The statement from the train driver said only that the body hit his windscreen from above. Forensic evidence, relative to point of impact confirmed the driver's story. There were no witnesses and no logical explanation. The body was eventually identified as one William John Smith, a 35-year-old petty criminal with several driving convictions to his credit. The inquest returned an open verdict. Nick said out loud, "how odd," and looked at the dates on the reports, just over a year ago.

The second folder was much more recent. Three months ago, a woman had called the police claiming to have been assaulted. Two police officers were sent to investigate. Upon arrival at the house they found an elderly woman in a wheelchair in a state of extreme distress. The officer in charge estimated the woman to be in her mid to late seventies, and based upon information obtained from the woman, the officer summoned the woman's doctor. Despite further investigation at the scene, the woman could produce no evidence of an assault, physical or otherwise. She could give no description of her attacker. There was no evidence of either a break in or disturbance.

The officers stayed with the woman until the doctor arrived to treat her. The doctor did what he could but claimed not to know the lady in question and stated quite categorically that she was not a patient of his. His patient was a single woman, an actress apparently, by the name of Sue Ann Mackenzie, 37 years old and of American extraction. However the address was the same.

The old woman claimed to be Sue Ann Mackenzie but no corroborating evidence could be produced to verify the claim. Neighbours claimed never having seen the old woman before that day. The last positive sighting of the real Sue Ann Mackenzie was the previous day at a small local theatre where she had a small part in a play in rehearsal there.

The old woman, still making claims as to her identity was placed in a hospital, under psychiatric care.

Sue Ann Mackenzie remains registered missing.

Nick closed the folders and pushed them back into the envelope. "Just what the hell is going on here? First the video tape now this." He looked at the big envelope containing the files. The label was typed and self adhesive, the post mark was yesterday.

"Somebody somewhere is trying to tell me something, but what?"

There was no correlation between the cases he had just read about, except that they were bizarre in the extreme. And they certainly did not have any connection with the video. But instinctively he surmised there must be a connection because his gut told him that as strange as it seemed, both the items had come from the same person.

While he sat mulling these things over in his mind he resolved to do one thing as soon as it could be arranged, and that was to seek out Professor Harman-Jones. Previously he had been ready to dismiss the video as an interesting side event, something that an unknown acquaintance had sent him in the thought that it might amuse him. Now something told him he needed to meet the man and learn a little more about him and his strange claims.

Come Monday morning, with the resources of the police force at his command, it didn't take long to locate the professor. It transpired that he had a seat at St. Mary's College... in Cambridge no less. Of course coming up with a suitable excuse to go there would prove more of a challenge. However his mind was jolted back to earth by a knock on his office door. The uniformed sergeant, who stuck his head round the door at his muffled yell to come in, said, "I've got a Superintendent Hodges to see you, sir," and he stood aside to usher a tall uniformed man inside.

Nick stood up and came to meet his unexpected guest. "DCI Burton... how can I help you, sir?"

They shook hands warmly. "I'll come straight to the point, Burton. I have been given the unenviable task of looking into this business concerning your old boss. I've no idea how long it's going to take but I will need an office of some sort while I'm here."

Nick smiled. "Unenviable indeed, he was well liked and still nobody around here can believe any of its true."

"Including you?"

"Especially me, sir. He was a friend and mentor as well as my boss."

"I understand, but still…"

"As far as an office is concerned you might as well use this one. I haven't really moved in yet and to be honest it doesn't really fit me."

"Only if you're sure… I have no intention of throwing your station into chaos I'm just looking for some answers, alright if I start with you?"

"Fire away," replied Nick, "but don't you want to settle in, what about staff or some tea or coffee?"

"I've an Inspector cooling his heels in your canteen. I'd like to bring him up and he can bring the drinks with him, if you can give him a call?"

Once the Inspector had arrived and the introductions had been made, they let Nick fill them in on what he knew, which he confessed was no more than anybody else.

Nick concluded with, "I'm sorry, sir. I know you've a job to do and all that, but there's nothing to find. I've been having a look and the only thing Colin Murray and Dan Davies had in common was they were both victims of a robbery that took place fifteen years ago."

"I understand that, Burton, but our leaders are fearful of their pensions and what the media will say if we don't put out some sort of release soon. What with the funeral coming up that's bound to stir the story up again."

The funeral, it had escaped Nick's mind, so caught up was he with his own investigations. He smiled inwardly, what bloody investigations? You're no further ahead than these two. "I agree, sir, but God alone knows what we're going to say."

Jenny Smythe, Dan's daughter, had sent him an email saying that she was arriving over the weekend and she was going to stay at her dad's house. The funeral was scheduled for Thursday morning.

He made a note to himself to get over to the house and see her, make sure the local press hacks were not around. Obviously because of the circumstances there was no way the funeral could in any way be the formal police event it should be. That really would be asking for trouble, but everybody he had spoken to had said they were going, officially or not.

Then as if someone had slapped him hard in the face, he thought: Burton you are a dull bugger sometimes! Funerals, what about Colin Murray's funeral? What about his family? No one, as far as he knew had given them a second thought. Perhaps they knew something that could give him a new lead.

"Mary!" he shouted out for DC Riley who appeared like a genie. "Mary, find out about Colin Murray's funeral. Has it taken place yet? What about his family, where they are now, has anybody seen them since?" Words failed him.

"Since he was murdered, sir? I don't know, give me some time and I'll find out," and again genie like she disappeared.

It wasn't long before she was back, knocking on his door. He looked up expectantly. A quick look at her note pad and she said, "Funeral's all over, it was Friday last week. Local paper did a small bit about it but it was well buried. His parents still live locally they've got a small semi on Douglas Road."

"Good job, now go get your coat and let's go see if they're in to callers."

"Sir?" It was a question.

"If for no other reason than to offer our condolences… I don't know, I'd like to meet them. I never met their son perhaps they can give us a clue why anyone would want to kill him."

By the time they got there it was nearly lunch time Nick rang the door bell and waited, warrant card in hand. It seemed no one was at home. He rang the bell again and this time he heard a door inside close with a bang and there were feet on the stairs. The inside door opened and a woman's shape appeared through the frosted glass. As she opened the outside door Nick said "Mrs. Murray, I'm Chief Inspector Burton from the local CID and this is DC Riley. May we talk to you for a few minutes?"

The woman who stood before them was small in stature and almost gaunt in appearance. Her thin grey hair was pulled back from her forehead and tied in a no nonsense bun at the back. There was no visible sign of recognition no smile or grimace, nothing. She just stood there, looking not at them but through them. A voice from inside shouted, "Who the hell is it? If they're selling anything tell 'em to bugger off, I want me dinner."

"It's the police," she said in a voice almost as lifeless as her appearance, "they want a word."

"What the hell do they want?" The man's voice started as a shout but it got closer as he spoke. When he came into sight Nick took an instant dislike to him, all his years in the force summed the man up in a single glance. The man who slouched into view was untidy in his appearance a stained vest was all that covered his upper body. His hair was in need of care and he looked as if he had not washed or shaved in days. He held an open newspaper in one hand, The Racing Times, if Nick was any judge, and as he got closer he asked again, "So what do you want? We was just going to sit down to dinner."

Nick suppressed the urge to laugh, an image of a butler serving dinner sprung uninvited into his minds eye. "Just a few words, if we may. We won't take up too much of your time, I promise."

Begrudgingly the man stood aside and let them in. "Better shove it in the oven, you know how I hate cold food,"

His wife shuffled off without a word. They followed Mr. Murray into the living room, which to Nick's surprise was extremely neat and tidy accept the corner where Mr. Murray threw himself into an over-stuffed armchair. "So speak, I haven't got all day."

With a casual look around Nick wanted to ask what urgent social engagement could possibly be so high on Mr. Murray's agenda, but he refrained from doing so. As Mrs. Murray made no attempt to join them Nick looked at Mary and nodded in the direction of the kitchen. She took the hint immediately and eased herself out of the room. If Mr. Murray noticed he made no comment.

"It's about your son Colin, sir, and before we start can I offer my condolences on your loss."

There was a loud snort from the corner. "About my son... It's always about my bloody son and you can shove your condolences where the sun don't shine..."

"Nevertheless, sir, I am deeply sorry for your loss."

"Loss... loss... What bloody loss? He was a vegetable for Christ's sake, the only bloody reason you're sorry is 'cos it was one of your lot that done him in. Bloody sue the lot of you so we should. Don't suppose that's why you're here, is it to offer us a pittance in compensation?"

"No Mr. Murray, that's not why I'm here, but if you want to make a formal complaint I can arrange for a….."

"Nah! Why bother, done us bloody favour if you ask me! You can see what it did for his mother, poor cow. So what do you want?"

Nick was really warming to the man. "I just wanted to ask you if you can think of any reason why anyone would want to kill your son, anything, anything, at all might help me?"

"How the hell should I know? I stopped going up the hospital years ago, his mother went regular stupid bitch, much good it did her. Nah! Like I said your mate did us a favour, maybe we can get on with life now."

Somehow Nick doubted that anything would change in the Murray household but he thanked Mr. Murray for his time and he gathered Mary from the kitchen and they left.

There was a pub at the end of the road and Nick took Mary for lunch.

"So how did you get on with Mrs. Murray? Better than I did with her husband, I hope?"

"I felt sorry for her, sir. She hasn't had much of a life, has she…First with the accident… and then finally losing her son and that god awful man."

"Quite!"

"She said she had to keep going, it was her duty. Nobody else would go near him apparently."

"What do you mean?"

"Oh! I don't know… she was very vague, seems the doctors and nurses made up stories about her son.

Stupid things, like he was creepy and could do things with his eyes. Nobody ever wanted to be alone in the room with him, especially the nurses and more especially at night."

"How odd, did she say anything else?"

"Not really, she's very hard to get anything out of, if you know what I mean?"

"Well, I guess you'd better go to the hospital and have a poke around. Talk to the nurses and see what you can scare up, if that's the right word."

Back at the station Nick walked into a room full of gloomy people. "Christ, what's up with you lot?"

"Stringer got off on a technicality. The judge let him go! He's back on the streets as we speak."

Tony Stringer was the local crime lord and head of the Stringer clan. Three generations of a large family that terrorised an entire neighbourhood and had their dirty little fingers into to all aspects of crime. If the Stringers were not involved then it didn't happen. If it did happen then you could expect to find hospital emergency rooms suddenly filling up with people with missing or badly bent body bits. Old man Stringer and Dapper Dan were old sparring partners. Dan had been responsible for putting quite a few of the Stringers and their various relatives behind bars, but he never got the old man. There had been a sort of grudging respect between the two of them. At least while old man Stringer was in control, the entire area was free of drugs. But his eldest son Tony was a completely different character; he was into anything that made money.

Nick replied, "What! We worked day and night for six bloody months... how the hell?"

DS Martin replied, "One of the prosecution's key witnesses changed his story in the box. Got his days mixed up, couldn't have been where he said he was. He was off sick that day. He'd been knobbled."

Nick was furious. "Well of course he'd been bloody knobbled! Question is how…he was supposed to have been in protective custody…."

"He was in custody but while he was in the cells below the court, something happened."

"Like what?" Nick asked.

"Afterwards we found a mobile phone in his cell. There was a text message on it saying, the insurance policy on his wife had expired."

"Did you at least trace the call?"

"There was no call, in or out. The phone was brand new, never used, just the one message typed on it."

Nick sighed. "Just when you thought it couldn't get any worse… Now I suppose I'll have the Chief Constable all over my backside."

"So boss, what do we do now?"

"Do? Do? We start all over again, that's what we do. I want that son of a bitch locked up and as many of his family as we can get. One by one if we have to, but get them we will."

Nick was still seething when Mary Riley got back from the hospital and stuck her head round his door. "I'm only in if its good news."

"I bring gifts," she replied showing him a large cup of shop bought coffee.

In spite of his mood, he smiled and waved her in. Besides, it wasn't her fault that the scourge of the district was back on the streets, or as to why he sometimes questioned exactly whose side the law was really on. "What you got?"

Mary sat down and started, "You are not going to believe it... this is straight out of the Twilight Zone."

Nick looked over the desk at her. "You don't look old enough to remember the Twilight Zone."

"I got Satellite. Anyway, it seems as though it's not only Mr. Murray senior that thinks DCS Davies did him a favour. Most of the nursing staff is pretty glad to see the back of Murray junior as well."

"You'll have to explain that to me. The man was paralysed from the eyebrows, he couldn't speak and he was practically brain dead, so why...?"

"That's just it, sir. He wasn't brain dead, far from it in fact. His brain was one of the few things that actually worked... too well, by all accounts. They reckon that he was using his brain power to do things."

"Oh come on! Like what?"

"Things would happen in the room, like lights going on and off, objects falling over for no good reason, doors opening or closing by themselves or getting stuck switching TV channels that sort of thing."

"You're not serious, are you?"

" I told you it was Twilight Zone stuff. I'm just telling you what they said, and trust me they weren't smiling when they spoke. One nurse said she was trapped in the room one night, she went in to check on his vital signs and the door blew closed and the lights went off. She said she tried the door but it was locked or stuck and when she banged on it there was no sound. Another nurse said she was groped in that room."

"Who by?... surely you're not suggesting Colin Murray, for God's sake?"

"She swears that she felt a hand fondle her breasts and move slowly down her body to her inner thigh. Apparently she threatened to quit her job if they ever made her go back into that room while he was there. That's not all, they said he could control his heart rate, kinda slow it down."

"Again I ask why?"

"Main theory is, it was to attract attention if the heart stops or becomes irregular. It triggers an alarm and brings everyone running."

Nick let go an enormous sigh. "My god Mary, the deeper we get into this thing the more bizarre it becomes. None of it makes any sense whatsoever. And now you bring me this… this… psychic mumbo jumbo… What the hell do I say to the Chief Constable? DCS Davies killed Colin Murray to stop him from mentally groping his nurses?"

Mary looked across the desk at him her face was deadly serious. "I don't understand any of it either, but I'll tell you this, for what its worth. Those nurses believe it happened and it scared them. I don't know a thing about psychosomatic doings, I don't even know if that's the right word, but there is definitely a connection there somewhere."

Nick dragged his hands through his hair; "Perhaps you're right, I don't know, it's well out of our league. Thanks Mary, good effort, I just wish to hell I could say it helped."

As Mary left the room Nick just sat back in his chair and spun from side to side. One thing's for sure, he thought, I need to speak to this professor Jones. Maybe he can make sense of it all because I am buggered if I can.

Thursday morning came, and dressed in his best suit and black tie, Nick made his way across town to Dan Davies's old house. As he reached for the bell the door was pulled open and a complete stranger stood before him blocking his path. A voice from behind the stranger said, "Nick, come in," and Dan's daughter Jenny appeared by the inner door. "Darling, this is Nick Burton, dad's right hand man. Nick, this is my husband Jonathan, he only arrived late last night."

The two men sized one another up at a glance and shook hands warmly in spite of the circumstances. Jenny looked radiant and they made a handsome looking couple.

"Sorry about being a bit brisk, thought you was another one of those press Johnnies."

"I'm sorry too," replied Nick, "I thought I'd taken care of them. Don't worry, I'll get uniform to put a couple of men out here, get them pushed back to a respectful distance."

Nick turned to Jenny and took her hand. "So how are you holding up? Anything I can do before we go?"

She smiled at him and with her husband standing protectively close by her shoulder, she replied, "You know what I want... no not want... need, is for you to clear my father's name. He was no murderer this is so ridiculous."

Nick's face was set. "Jenny, I told you the other night, I'm looking into it but you have to accept the fact that he actually confessed. He even threw me out of the cell when I tried to see him he didn't want anyone else to get involved."

Jenny held up her hands in mock surrender, "Ok! Ok! I hear you but I don't believe it. If everyone is so sure then why can't any of you tell me why?"

"Because we don't know why, and that's the God's honest truth. I'm trying to find out but the more I find the less I know."

Jonathan smiled weakly at Nick as he steered Jenny away; this was serving no purpose and was just upsetting everyone. As Nick looked around the room, it was in total silence, and all eyes were upon them. Naturally they all tried to hide their eyes as Nick looked at them and an unnatural buzz of conversation started up to cover their embarrassment.

When they got to the church Nick was not surprised to see that it was packed to capacity. What did surprise him was the number of police uniforms on show. This was contrary to the official instructions put up on the notice board and seemed to have been ignored by quite a few officers, among them Deputy Chief Constable Hardcastle.

The second shock he got was when he noticed how many of the opposition were also present. Ok, not your more recent villains but some from the old school, many of whom, Nick was sure, had had a taste of prison life, courtesy of the man they were here to bury.

One late arrival took him completely unawares. Accompanied by two younger people was none other than professor Harman-Jones. He looked much older than he had in the video and he was now in a wheelchair. The girl fussed at him trying to tuck a tartan travelling rug around his legs. While the professor armed with a walking stick urged them onwards at a swift pace.

Nick wasn't sure if he was intrigued or annoyed. He felt this was like being part of a giant jig-saw puzzle without a picture. It didn't even have any defining edges. But as if guided by an unseen hand, bit by bit things seemed to be falling… if not into place …at least they appeared to be the right way up for a change. With this latest piece he was now absolutely sure that the video tape, the mysterious files and the murder of Colin Murray were all linked and this funny old man was the key.

After the funeral there was a gathering of sorts. At least many of those attending the funeral were now in the large function room of a nearby hotel, sipping sherry or tea and making embarrassingly polite conversation.

Nick was trying his best to get into the small group that contained the professor, hovered over by his overly protective assistants. He was obviously a popular man, something of a local celebrity, so it struck him as odd that in all the years he and Dan had worked together no mention of the professor ever came up.

In desperation Nick picked up a plate and brazenly pushed his way into the huddle, offering sandwiches to all and sundry as he went. Once in the middle he grabbed the opportunity of a lull in the conversation to introduce himself.

"Professor Harman-Jones, my name is Nick Burton...." He could see the professor's minders heading to cut him off. "Detective Chief Inspector Nick Burton, I was Chief Superintendent Davies's number two."

The hounds still came forward but at a gentler pace. "Could we have a word, would you mind?"

The professor smiled up at him. He had lost none of his hair in the ten years since the video was made and along with his beard it was as wild and unruly as ever. Those thick lenses in their dark frame made him look like a wise old owl peering from within a grey thicket.

"Of course my boy, of course... Don't mind these two, they're a tad overprotective but I indulge them."

Nick suspected the old rogue rather enjoyed the attention.

"Let me introduce them," he held up his hand and the woman came over and took it. "This is Doctor Jill Tindell, Jilly to her friends, and the gent lurking behind her is Alan Redman... former students of mine and now my closest associates."

Nick took Jilly's hand and for some strange reason was pleased to see that although she wore rings on her fingers a wedding band was not one of them. He said, "Doctor Tindell pleased to meet you," and he looked into a pair of the greenest eyes he had ever seen.

Her handshake was warm and firm and she seemed to hold his hand for just a little too long, or was that just wishful thinking on his part? "Chief Inspector," she replied, "Sorry about the reception. We thought you were one of those awful press people."

Nick looked alarmed. "Are they here? Point them out to me and I'll have them removed immediately."

Another hand came his way. "Alan Redman," said the man. "I don't think they're actually here in the hall but they were definitely outside the church. Look, if you want Jilly and I to push off..."

"No. No not at all," Nick replied, "it's nothing like that... more curiosity than anything. I just wanted to enquire why you are here, and to ask for your connection to Dan. That's all."

The professor answered with an owlish grin, "He was one of my students, one of the best ever as I recall. I'm Sorry to see him go. Now we'll have to start all over again."

Nick was flabbergasted. "You mean he was a current student? Not someone from the old days when he was at college?"

"Dan Davies was helping us with some of our most exciting and comprehensive experiments ever and now…now …it's over... such a shame…"

The professor's head slumped forward onto his chest. Jilly pushed passed Nick. "Look inspector, this is going too far, it will have to wait."

Nick wanted to protest. Experiments, what experiments, into what? But he just said, "I understand. But this is rather important… it's just that …"

She was kneeling at the side of the wheelchair and she looked up at him. Those green eyes were piercing but her expression softened as she saw the pain on his face. She put her hand into her coat pocket and pulled out a small business card and held it out to him.

"Maybe I can help you get the answers you seek at least some of them, but it will have to be in Cambridge alright? Give me a call when you're ready, but come with an open mind."

As he took the card he gazed deep into those eyes, he tried to hold eye contact with her but her attention was back with her charge. "Now please, if you'll excuse us, we must go."

As he watched the back of the three receding figures he caught a hint of her voice, "I knew we shouldn't have come….." It faded as they left the room. He thought: was that a reference to him? Had he caused the professor undue anxiety or was his probing getting too close into their research?

He looked again at her card, Dr. Jill Tindell, and a string of letters longer than her name. Doctor of what he wondered as he put the card in a safe place?

"Damn pretty gal, that." Nick didn't need to turn round to recognise the gruff tone of DCC Hardcastle.

"Indeed yes, sir I must admit I had similar thoughts."

"So Burton, I know this is neither the time nor the place but are you making any progress with this Davies thing? I mean, you are looking into it, aren't you?"

"Oh yes, sir. I'm looking into it alright, but so far I'm not having much success. It's like trying to straighten worms, if you know what I mean? I worked with the man for years, went to his house for dinner, watched Jenny over there grow up and get married. I stood by him as best I could when Patricia died but I have to admit sir, I don't think I really knew him at all."

"Quite so, quite so... I understand, always a blow when you lose a chum and all that but you were closer to him than anybody. Don't give up on him, there's a good chap."

"Give up, sir? No, I won't do that, I promise you. If there's a reason I will find it."

"Good man, now if you'll excuse me I'm off to find the bar. This sherry is all well and good but too much of the stuff rots your innards, don't you know?"

Nick wasn't sure if it was pure duty or common courtesy, but he was one of the last to leave the reception. He had seen his staff and most of the others from his station come and go as their duties allowed. But as the rest of the mourners drifted away he moved closer to Jenny and Jonathan and again offered, "If there's anything I can do…"

Jenny took his hand, her eyes were red. Nick understood all too well. These occasions were like a hell on earth for those closest to the departed. Everyone wanted to say how sorry they were and share a favourite story. We all did it, like some sort of selfish right of passage.

She replied, "Jonathan will be going home tomorrow. His duties won't allow him to stay, but I'll stay around for a few days more. We'll be selling the house, so I need to get everything packed up and moved out. If there's anything there you want... you know... a memento or something...."

"Jenny, if you need a hand all you have to do is say, OK? I'll call you tomorrow. Maybe we can go out to dinner or something."

She said nothing, just squeezed his hand. Jonathan stretched out his hand and shook Nick's hand very firmly and the two men turned towards the door. "You will take care of her for me, if it's not asking too much?"

"I will, don't worry."

Nick walked for a long time. He walked until his mind came back to earth and he realised he had no idea where he was and above all he was starving. He jumped onto a bus and headed for the town centre and a favourite Indian restaurant. In spite of himself and all that was going on around him, all he could manage to think about was a very pretty woman with impossibly green eyes.

A late night taxi took him home and as he closed the front door of the block of flats there on the little table was a package for him. As he picked it up, he felt the telltale signs of another video tape. His immediate reaction was one of anger. *What is this? It's like some sort of Chinese water torture: Drip, Drip, Drip... a little piece here, a little piece there.* He looked at the front of the package. The same tidy computer printed label.

Same type of envelope as before, but this time there was neither post mark nor stamps.

This had been delivered by hand. Someone out there knows a bloody sight more than they are letting on. They are playing me like a puppet and when I find out who…...

Chapter 4

Once in the comfort of his flat, Nick tossed the small package onto the settee and he went into the bedroom stripped off and took a shower. One way or another it had been quite a day, saying farewell to an old friend, meeting professor Harman-Jones and his lovely assistant, and finally getting another package.

It was like standing naked in a hot hail storm. The steam whirled around him as the jets of water hit his shoulders, like demented fingers determined to rid him of the aches of the day. In this tiny haven from the world he relaxed and let his mind wander.

Soon he could see her again, the gentle smile and those eyes. Just as quickly he could feel the tension return as he thought of that package sitting unopened in the next room. Right now all he wanted to do was to finish his shower and fall into bed but he knew that was not going to happen. Bed and sleep were impossible until the contents of that tape were revealed.

He wanted coffee but settled for tea, as he powered up the TV and video player popped the tape into the slot and settled back on the settee pressing the play button as he went.

This time there was no amateurish fumbling around. The screen was immediately a bright blue and a voice said, "Sound test, one, two, three, three, two, one."

Then on screen came a face instantly recognisable to him; it made his blood run cold because it was like watching a ghost appear. The image of Dan Davies sat there behind a clear desk with nothing but a blank wall behind him. The face of his old friend smiled at him.

"Hello Nick! I'm sorry for the dramatics, but let me assure you that all of this is for the best and was designed to protect you and others in what happened. I am also sorry for sending you on a wild goose chase to Cardiff, knowing your love of travel, but I wanted to make absolutely sure you had a cast iron alibi. One strong enough and obvious enough that not even Superintendent Joy could miss."

"The fact that you are seeing this at all means that, for me at least, it's all over. If I have left a mess, then again, I apologise. Believe me it was not intentional. Yes, there will be confusion, but I intended only to solve a major problem in a way that gave them an open and shut case, no messy court appearances and minimal embarrassment to the force. Yes, there will be questions and possibly media interest but as always this will undoubtedly die down with time. If there had been any other way, trust me, I would have taken it."

"Look out for Jenny for me. I know she's married now to Jonathan, he's a good man at heart but his career sometimes clouds his better judgement. There will be times when she might need the services of a friend."

"I don't suppose there is any point in telling you not to go poking around for answers as to why the old man flipped in such a major way, but I'll tell you anyway. No real good can come of it, and I doubt you will find a conclusion that you can accept."

"Let the official record show that I committed a terrible crime while the balance of my mind was unstable. Call it severe depression, following the death of my wife. God knows that's true enough and that I

then committed suicide for the same reason. Least said, soonest mended."

"Goodbye, my dear friend. I enjoyed the many years we spent working together. You're a good detective and a good policeman. Have patience these things will be rewarded."

"Please don't think too badly of me."

And as these words were spoken Dan's face faded away and the screen returned to blue.

Nick rewound the tape and watched it again, tears rolling down his cheeks. If he was looking for answers or clues there was none here, just confirmation of what had happened and a note of farewell. As he watched that final blue screen for the second time all he could feel was sorrow, sorrow for the meaningless loss of a good man. The question that came to mind was, had some external and as yet unknown somebody been jerking Dan's chain as well?

He went to bed, not one step closer to the truth, disappointed and angry.

The following day he was in a bad mood. His head ached and he was generally at war with the world. DS Dave Martin, who had caught the full blast, came back into the outer CID office sheepishly rubbing his backside and said, "God help any criminal who gets in his way today! Everything's in his way but his own backside."

Mary Riley jumped to Nick's defence. "Give him some space, for Christ sake! He's just buried his best friend and besides you did screw up."

Dave retorted, "I thought you were his new best friend... Friendly lunches, secret cups of coffee..."

She stuck her tongue out at him. "Jealousy will get you nowhere."

At first Nick wanted to follow him and apologise and then thought: bugger it, he deserved it and if it gives me peace and quiet today then so much the better.

He tried to clear his mind and review everything he knew about the case. "What case?" he asked himself. That bloody professor is at the bottom of all this, I'll bet my pension on it. It's like that movie, what was it called? *The Manchurian Candidate*, all about deep hypnosis or brain washing, or something like that. Was that the experiments they were up to?

"Nah!'"

He dismissed it out of hand. Dan would never be party to anything like that. But what if he didn't know? Let's face it, that's what the whole bloody movie was about, not knowing.

But even so… If that sort of thing went on in this country, surely it would be very hush, hush. Not something they would prat around with at Cambridge. There is a sort of twisted, devious logic there, get someone with a totally unblemished record to go out and kill someone for no known reason, confess and then conveniently die. Makes sense of all the facts, leak it to the press, think of the headline:

"Manchurian Candidate style experiments at Cambridge.

Nutty professor and his green eyed female accomplice arrested."

As he scanned his meagre notes for the umpteenth time he came once more to one of the earliest things he had written down, it was something that Dan had said:

'Go home and stay there, everything you need to know is there.'

At some point he had even underlined it.

It was not until now that he even gave the statement any thought at all. He had literally dismissed it as Dan's attempt to keep him out of things. But this time he read it aloud and then, as he did so, the full significance hit him. Of course, **Home.... Everything you need...** It had been a message, not an instruction. So far everything that had helped him move forward had been delivered to his home, the tapes, the folders. Then he thought would there be something tonight? If there was it would confirm that there was indeed a mysterious Mr. X out there, playing him like a fish on a line. But why all this cloak and dagger shit? Why not just come forward and lay all the cards on the table?

Not finding answers to these and a hundred other questions didn't improve his mood. The day progressed steadily downhill. He had a run in with the uniform boys, after what should have been a straight forward capture and arrest went horribly wrong and at least two suspects got clean away.

One of his team had crashed his car into another vehicle in an attempt to prevent a getaway, only to find out it was the wrong car. And to top it all Mary Riley, trying her best to help sooth things down, collided head on with him in the passage, drenching them both in hot coffee. Following that incident he stormed out of the building and was gone.

He wanted to go home, fearing that another envelope would be there waiting for him. But what if it wasn't? It was almost drug like in its effect and he was becoming addicted. If it was there....no.., no... if it was not there, what would he do then? He needed these clues he was making no progress on his own. Alone he was not going to solve this one. For some reason someone out there was drip feeding him the answers he sought, the why was no longer important, only the desire to get there.

Grabbing a Chinese take-away on the way, he headed for his flat - worrying what might be there, scared that there would be nothing there at all. But as he pushed open the door, his neighbour on the ground floor came scurrying out to greet him. An elderly woman with a love of cats, she had at least six to his knowledge even although the tenancy agreement forbade pets, except caged birds, for some obscure reason.

"Mr. Burton! Oh there you are, I've been so worried I'd missed you, you keep such odd hours, you know," as if she was telling him something he didn't already know.

"Miss. Finch, how are you? Your cats they are all well, I trust?"

She looked as though she was about to go in full little old lady mode when he skilfully intercepted her as she was warming up.

"You have something for me?"

"Why yes, how odd that you would guess that, but of course you are a detective, aren't you? It reminds me that I once went walking out with a policeman. We used to go down to the park on a beautiful Sunday morning after church and …"

"The package, or was it an envelope, Miss. Finch?"

The old dear came back to reality with a little shudder. "Such a nice gent… what… Oh yes, the package.. Now where did I put it? One of those young men on a motorcycle… Or was it a young woman, you can never tell these days can you?"

"Miss Finch, the package! I don't mean to be rude but my dinner is getting cold," and he held up the carrier bag in emphasis.

She took the hint and without further ado produced the now familiar envelope. As soon as he took it into his hand he realised at once it was another tape.

"Thank you, thank you so much. I'm very grateful to you," and he started up the stairs two at a time.

The words, "you're very welcome, I'm sure," receded behind him.

All thoughts of his dinner went out of his head, his long suffering microwave oven would solve that problem later, as he tore open the envelope. The tape tumbled onto the floor in his haste to get to the machine. He fumbled it into place and started punching buttons on the remote control unit.

As he took off his coat and jacket he wondered what it would be this time, another lecture from the professor or something all together different. He didn't have to wait long the TV hissed with static and then went silent as the screen turned blue and the familiar face of Dan Davies appeared for the second time.

"So you've met the professor."

It was not a question it was more like a statement of fact.

"Interesting chap got some really whacky ideas about the ultimate mode of travel but other than that he's quite genuine and down to earth."
"I don't know how you two met, bad luck, or you ignored my suggestion to leave well alone, or just sheer coincidence... Doesn't really matter now... However,

before you go stomping over toes I suppose I had better give you the gist of it."

"One thing I never told you. I don't know why, but fourteen, fifteen years ago I got myself shot; damn silly really. Anyway, together with a detective sergeant I was on observation duty, helping out the drug squad as I remember, been there off and on for days. Boring as hell but then we got this shout about a robbery in progress at a jewellers in the High Street. Just round the corner from where we were."

"As luck would have it, one of the drug guys was there so we left him to it and we legged it to the High Street. As we arrived all hell seemed to be breaking loose, the alarm had gone off, there was a lot of shouting and I saw two men coming out of the jeweller's pushing a wheelchair, of all things, and dragging a bloke in some sort of uniform behind them. Then for some apparent reason the dull bugger I was with shouted: **"Armed Police! Stop and Give Yourselves up**.*"*

"Neither of us was actually armed, but the challenge had been made. One of the two robbers turned and pointed a gun in our direction. I saw smoke and felt a hell of a pain in my leg, I stumbled... heard the shot...Then nothing."

"I suppose one of the reasons I never spoke about the incident, not just to you but anybody, is the embarrassment of what I am about to reveal. You and everybody else around me have always seen me as I wanted to be seen: calm, a level headed, feet firmly planted on the ground sort of a chap. Too much the detective, I couldn't accept what couldn't be proven. There were no real mysteries, only situations where some of the facts were missing. So what I am about to

tell you shook everything I had previously believed to the core. Although, I'll admit, at the time it all seemed quite natural."

"Even now it's hard. For instance, I don't know if what I'm saying now is how I felt at the time or it's how I have analysed and rationalised it all to myself all these years.

However, I honestly feel that at the time I thought I was dead. I also thought how unconcerned I felt about the fact."

"There I was thirty, forty feet above the scene looking down at my sergeant tearing off his jacket balling it up and putting it beneath my head. As I turned I could see a blue Jaguar taking off down the street scattering jaywalkers as it went. It turned right and headed for the London Road, I remember feeling slightly annoyed at the fact that I had lost sight of it. Then for some reason I remembered where I was and without effort I floated higher until I could see the car speeding ahead of me. I could now see a police car on an intercept course, blue lights blazing. I even remember the large black Call Letters 'CF' on the car's roof."

"Charlie Foxtrot almost made it to the roundabout first, there could only have been seconds in it. No matter, he was now right behind the Jag, hammering down the London Road dual carriageway, weaving in and out of the traffic. I could imagine the crew of Charlie Foxtrot giving a running commentary as they sped after them directing other cars to intercept. At one of the roundabouts the Jag heaved left onto one of the other exit roads. I can't remember if another car had blocked their path to the London Road exit or not, but the move blindsided the crew of Charlie Foxtrot and

they had to go right round the roundabout before they could take up the chase again."

"By God, chase them they did! I've never seen such driving, it seemed only minutes before they were right on the tail of the Jag once more. It was then that I saw it, a few hundred yards ahead there was a car parked at the side of the road, obviously with a flat rear tyre because a young man was kneeling down in the road completely unaware at what was right behind him. He must have heard the siren of Charlie Foxtrot because first he looked around and then he started to move. Too late, the Jaguar was upon him, the driver braked far too late and way too hard. The car went into a skid, the driver releasing the brake to correct the cars direction. It hit that young man so hard it threw him in the air like a rag doll."

"There was no choice, the Jaguar slowed down but the driver soon regained control and gunned the engine and sped away, but Charlie Foxtrot had to stop. Even if they could have got past the broken body lying in the road they were duty bound to stop and render immediate assistance, which to their great credit they did."

"I saw it all unfold before my eyes as if it were nothing more than a movie on the television. I watched the disaster scene below me and I could also see the Jaguar speeding away up the valley and then turning down a country lane and head off cross country."

"Then the strangest thing happened. As I was watching this drama taking place, I had the strangest sensation that I was no longer alone. There beside me was the very image of the guy on the ground. We both just watched the scene below us: the crew of Charlie Foxtrot taking charge, blocking off the road, calling for

back-up, organising an ambulance. It never occurred to either of us to try and speak, at least it didn't occur to me and as he didn't make any effort to communicate. I didn't try either. I just floated there watching and waiting, for what I didn't know."

"It wasn't until I saw the ambulance approaching that I gave my own situation any thought at all. I looked around; the town was laid out before me like a toy. It was as if I had my own silent helicopter. I could go wherever I wanted. In the blink of an eye I was back over the High Street, needless to say there were blue lights and people everywhere. But upon closer examination all the blue lights were police cars, there was no ambulance there. I floated down to get a better look of the crime scene and to my amazement the body was gone, my body."

"Again I floated skywards, scanning the distance and there, heading logically enough towards the hospital, was an ambulance, lights flashing, siren blaring. Instantly I was inside that ambulance. My God, what a mess, there was blood everywhere! The ambulance guy was standing over me talking, telling me to hang on, that was the first inkling that I had that I wasn't actually dead. The sergeant was there too, jacketless with his shirt covered in blood. I assumed that as nobody was looking his way the blood must all be mine."

"Everything you see on these TV programmes is real. The ambulance crew must have radioed ahead, because as we arrived at the hospital and screeched to a halt, the rear doors were flung open and there were people everywhere. It seems ridiculous now but I got out first, I didn't want to be in the way. It was amazing, the effort these people were putting in to save me. I

agree I'm no expert in these things but when I looked down at the mess and all that blood I personally would have said: forget it guys, this one's a goner."

"I was still hovering around the emergency room when another ambulance arrived, this one carrying the victim of the hit and run that I had so recently witnessed. Miraculously he too was alive, but God alone knows why, the way he was tossed in the air and the way he landed I had been convinced that he was dead for sure."

"I could see that they were in the process of wheeling my body off to the operating theatre and I thought that perhaps I should tag along. I don't know why, they didn't seem to need me, not the floating me anyway, they seemed to be doing just fine."

"Do you see what I'm trying to explain to you? It was a completely different world, I knew what was happening, I could see everything, hear everything. I knew that it was my body lying on that table badly damaged, dying for all I knew, but in this world I was completely unconcerned. As I recall I was more outraged at the crimes I had witnessed than being shot."

"I remember drifting away through the corridors and back to the emergency rooms to check upon the young man who had been hit and I heard the list of injuries and broken bones being reeled off. I also remember them saying he might be better off if he did die, his chances of a full recovery were nil. They said that even if he did recover better than ninety-five percent of his body would be paralysed."

"I don't know what dragged me back to the operating theatre but I arrived there suddenly. I heard urgency in their voices that hadn't been there before.

One voice was counting off numbers... falling numbers, another voice said we're loosing him..."

"Then, all of a sudden I realised the part I had to play in this drama. From my lofty position all I had to do was to float down and tell myself to live."

There was no sound from the TV. Nick just stared at the image of his old friend clearly the retelling of this story had had quite an effect upon him. There was a telltale double blip on the screen that told Nick that the recording had been halted and then restarted later.

"The fact that I'm here, now, telling you all this means that it worked. Not immediately of course. I wandered in and out of my body several more times that day. I remember on one trip looking for my new friend, as I now thought of that poor injured young man. I found him floating above his own body looking down as I had done upon my own just seconds before. Although again we didn't speak I realised that he too was conscious of what was happening around him and like me he could see and hear the people who were attending him. I hadn't heard anyone say that I would be better off dead in the way they had said it over his broken body. I could only imagine how he must feel."

"I lay comatose for days. I can remember floating above myself several times, looking down and listening to the concerns being expressed about my condition. It wasn't until one particular visit from the doctors, summoned because of some sort of relapse that I heard one of them sigh and say, "There's nothing more we can do for him, it's all up to him now." It suddenly dawned on me that there was something they wanted me to do. I wasn't just some sort of mysterious

passenger along for the ride. There and then I decided no more flying around, fun though it was, you need to get better, and I did, two days later I was awake."

"The road to full recovery was long and for the most part painful and boring until, that is, one day two people came to see me, a young girl and I assumed her boyfriend.

I must have been dozing because it wasn't until I heard a voice say, we'll come back later, that I saw them hovering at the end of my bed. They looked so earnest; I took them for those religious freaks that hang around hospitals and was sorely tempted to keep my eyes closed. But I asked them to stay."

"They introduced themselves as Jilly Tindell and Alan Redman, students from Cambridge University, and they asked if I minded them asking a few questions. When I told them to go ahead, they started gingerly enquiring if anything strange had occurred over the period of my illness. I asked, such as? And they responded strange visions or anything like that."

"I must admit I got a bit shirty at that. It seemed to confirm my suspicions that they were from some sort of God squad or another looking for proof of whatever. But they had obviously been accused of this before and were all smiles and apologies. They told me a little more about themselves and that they were being deliberately vague so as not to prompt any false thoughts or suggestions in my head. I told them the story I have just told you. They were fascinated, hung upon my every word, tape recorder whirring away. It was the arrival of a nurse that put an end to the visit. They asked if they could come back after they had had a chance to talk to their professor. I readily agreed, the

relief from the monotony of hospital life was a welcome suggestion."

"Over the weeks they came back several times. I looked forward to their visits because their enthusiasm for their project was boundless. Of course by now they could reveal their studies revolved around what they called **Out of Body Experiences** *or alternatively* **Near Death Experiences.** *They seemed particularly interested in the fact that I had been conscious of another presence. A victim like me... not a deceased loved one come to guide me to the after life or an angel or something like that."*

"They apparently loved the fact that I was a detective and that I could stick to the facts without over embellishment. Without revealing names they told me about other investigations where the experiences of those involved became more elaborate with each telling of the story. There were tales of tunnels of light and the hand of God stretching out to guide them through. I saw nothing of the sort, of course that is not to say that is not what happened to others, perhaps I was not as close to death as I thought, who knows."

"The visits tailed off, I suppose there was nothing more to be gained from my experiences. They told me that their professor, a chap called Harman-Jones, wanted to meet me when I was up and about and they were gone. I missed them coming to see me, especially the girl, she had the most gorgeous green coloured eyes and she would sit holding my hand and hang upon my every word. The sort of girl you could so easily fall in love with."

"But a few months later I did hear from them again and Jilly offered to pick me up and take me to Cambridge for a day out. Patricia and I went together,

it was a fabulous spring day and we had a picnic lunch down on the riverside. Professor Harman-Jones was every inch what you would expect a professor to be, eccentric and enthusiastic in equal proportions. His wild un-kept appearance only added to his eccentricity, but he was passionate about his subject and it was obvious that he was adored by his students. He explained in great and glorious detail his theories about how little control we have over the power of our own brain. He used examples of out of body experiences, such as my own, to explain a futuristic means of transportation."

"He gave us details about how throughout our own brutal history we, in Western society, in the infinite arrogance of our own superiority, had so nearly wiped out the indigenous peoples of many lands. He cited the North American Indians, the Australian Aborigines and many of the tribal people of Africa. Within their folklore there are seers and shaman, soothsayers and mystics, who had for centuries conquered and understood the other world within, what he called Inner Space."

"Our illustrious forbearers called them savages and vowed to cure them of their heathen ways, little realising who the true and ignorant savages really were."

"He went on to thrill us with tales of monks in the high Himalayas who had mastered the art of levitation and telekinesis and other forms of psychic phenomena way beyond our comprehension. To be honest, as fascinating as I found his stories, he lost me on more than one occasion and in the short term I must admit I dismissed them as just that, stories. But he had something about him that gave you a hunger to learn

more. I was hooked over the many months convalescing I became a student, Patricia and I even rented a house nearer to Cambridge so that I could attend his lectures."

"Over the years, we became good friends. I confess I am nowhere near as convinced with his theories as some. Don't get me wrong, he is a passionate man and he is definitely onto something, but it will take smarter men than me to figure it out."

"So there you have it, the story behind the mysterious professor Harman-Jones. Sorry if it's not up to your expectations but there it is. I figured that if you ever found out about him you would simply worry yourself to death until you had worked it out. Now you don't have to bother. So why not just get on with your life forget about me and stop looking for conspiracies where none exists."

"Goodbye my friend."

Dan's face stayed on the screen for a few seconds more and then faded into the blue background. Nick just sat there staring at the screen. He ran everything he had just heard through his mind several times and from different angles and came to the following conclusion. With a wry grin on his face, the first in days he said aloud, "Nice try, Dan me boy, but wrong, this is just another piece of this infernal puzzle. If you really wanted me to back off you'd have told me why you did it. What did you call Colin Murray in the tape, your newfound friend, if he was your friend why did you think he needed killing?"

It was well past midnight when Nick put the Chinese takeaway in the fridge… untouched… and went to bed.

Just before sleep came there was one thing uppermost in his mind, come Monday he would be calling Dr. Jill Tindell to set up a meeting. With an image of those green eyes in his minds eye he fell asleep.

Thankfully for all concerned the weekend had been relatively quiet, so on Monday the entire CID office was pleased to see a more relaxed and cheerful Nick Burton. After morning prayers they broke up into their various assignments for that day.

Nick had a meeting with Superintendent Hodges and asked him how he was getting on and found out that he was not. On the surface there was literally nothing to find. The case, to all intents and purposes, was open and shut. It seemed that only the top brass were keeping it alive in some dumb effort to placate the news media, who, after the funeral seemed to have lost interest completely. Nick, on the other hand, was far from satisfied, a feeling he was not about to share with Superintendent Hodges.

He sat in his office but couldn't really settle to any specific task. He wondered, not for the first time, what would be a suitable moment to call the good doctor. For instance, what time did they start? Did they have a mid morning coffee break? What time was lunch? "Sod it," he said out loud and reached for the telephone, her business card was already on his desk. The phone was answered almost immediately.

"Professor Harman-Jones's department… Alan Redman speaking; how can I help you?"

Nick's heart sank. He was disappointed that the number she had given him was not her own private number. But there again, why should she? They had only met a couple of days ago at a funeral. He had so wanted it to be her, he would have even settled for her voice on an answering machine….

"Mr. Redman, I don't know if you remember me. It's Chief Inspector Burton, Thames Valley Police. We met the other day. I was kind of hoping to speak to Doctor Tindell." He tried to keep his voice as flat and professional as he could.

"She's actually in a lecture at this moment but I can interrupt her if it's important."

Little bastard is fishing, Nick thought. "No.. no please don't do that. But if I give you my number, perhaps you could get her to give me a call as soon as it's convenient. How is the professor, by the way, that was a nasty turn he had the other day."

"He's fine, thank you for asking. It's just that he will overdo things. He is more ill than he will admit! Both Jilly and I tried to talk him out of going all that way to the funeral but he insisted."

Jilly, he had referred to her by her pet name did that signify that they were more than working colleagues? "Can I enquire what is wrong with the professor, if it's not too rude a question?'

"He's suffering from motor neuron disease, and as you can imagine he hates every minute of it. Keeps telling us his work is far from over and he will not just sit back and wait for this disease to destroy him."

"Thank you for your help," Nick replied, passed him his phone number and hung up. He was still feeling a touch sorry for himself half an hour later when the phone rang. He snatched it out of the cradle.

"Burton."

"Is this a bad time? I can call back later, it's just they told me it was urgent."

It was her, like some sort of love sick school boy his heart was racing. If anybody had entered the room at that exact moment they would have seen him blushing. 'Sorry… I'm sorry," he stammered, "It's not a bad time, it's just my mind was somewhere else completely. How are you?"

Now he really was feeling embarrassed, what the hell are you thinking you're speaking to her like a long lost pal.

She laughed, "I'm fine, how are you?"

"Doctor Tindell, forgive me give me a moment to rearrange my feet in relation to my mouth."

There was that delicious little laugh again. "Will you please stop apologising? Now, what can I do for you?'

"Doctor Tindell, thank you for returning my call so promptly but I can assure you I never said it was urgent."

"The name is Jilly, or if you prefer Jill. Only my students call me Doctor Tindell, although it does come in handy for booking theatre tickets or last minute table reservations. All I was told that the Thames Valley Police wanted to talk to me urgently. I didn't twig who Chief Inspector Burton was until you spoke a second ago. I suspect it's somebody's idea of a good wind up putting the words Police and Urgent together in the same sentence. So how can I help?"

"Now that that is sorted out, do you remember offering me some answers to questions I hadn't even asked yet?"

There was a pause he could hear the amusement in her voice when she asked, "Is this an official police enquiry or are you just curious?"

"Does it need to be official? I'm just looking for information at this time."

"Do you need the answers bad enough to come to Cambridge, maybe buy a girl a drink?"

Now he knew she was teasing him. "I'm sure the police expenses could probably run to dinner, if that's acceptable to you and your family?"

"Sounds fine, but I caution you Chief Inspector, I'm not a cheap date, and I'm not married if that's what you were wondering."

"Please give me time, date and place. I assume there are good hotels in Cambridge if I need to spend the night."

"Inspector Burton, whatever are you suggesting…."

"Jill… Doctor Tindell, forgive me. I didn't…I didn't mean…"

The laugh at the other end of the line told him he had been well and truly had.

"I've a good mind to make you go Dutch for that."

She was still giggling slightly when she said, "Send me your email address and I'll get a room booked for you and send you the details."

"If that's not too much trouble."

"No trouble. We do it all the time for visiting dignitaries. Now I really must go, see you soon," and she hung up.

Bloody hell, he thought, talk about being out of your depth. I was not in control of that situation one little bit… and the notion both thrilled and frightened him at the same time. But in spite of that he had a date with the girl with green eyes and that filled him with a glowing satisfaction. He couldn't remember the last time he had been out with a woman. How sad was that?

Two whole days passed before her email arrived. Two days that passed very slowly for him. There were no more items delivered in the post and even that disappointed him. There was a hell of a lot missing from this case, and there was at least one someone out there that knew a damn sight more than he did.

The one thing that was pleasing was that in Jilly's Email she had chosen Friday night for their dinner. In his reply he tried to ask, as innocently as he could, if she was free at any other time during the weekend, just in case….

Her response was almost immediate: check your hotel reservation I made it for three nights, just in case…..

At morning prayers the following day he announced that he was going away for the weekend, leaving at lunch time on Friday and would not be back in the office until Monday morning. He finished with; "You have my mobile number should World War three break out."

Chapter 5

If you are smart, one thing you learn very early on in the police force is never, never tell anyone you are going on holiday or taking any time off until you are literally on your way out of the door. Nick Burton forgot that rule. So from bright and early on Friday morning until he threatened to shoot the next person through his door just before lunchtime, he was inundated with 'before you go's.'

So it was something of a relief to finally find himself at Kings Cross station and getting on a train, even for him. He was fairly relaxed about the whole affair, after all the entire journey from London to Cambridge was relatively short and when all was said and done it had been his own idea. Even so he surprised himself even more when he nodded off in the warm carriage. He awoke suddenly when a fellow passenger accidentally bumped his shoulder on his way passing by. He looked at his watch and was pleased to note that he only had five minutes to go to journeys end.

When he arrived at his hotel and was checking in, the receptionist handed him an envelope along with his key. As he moved away towards the rooms he opened the envelope and took out the note inside. In a very neat and legible hand he read:

"We're not dining in the hotel. I'll pick you up in reception at 7:30 Jilly"

Up in his room he re-read the note and worked out he had plenty of time for a leisurely shower and to change. He was sitting in the reception area a good ten minutes before appointment time, casually glancing through the old country magazines scattered on a glass topped occasional table. But at the same time he was well positioned to see the comings and goings through the main front door and to observe the activities of his fellow guests. He smiled to himself, you have been a bloody policeman for far too long, he thought.

One minute all was tranquil, an elderly couple over by reception seemed to be the only activity, when a cool breeze around his ankles told him the main door had just opened and there she was. Looking just as pretty as he remembered, only this time she was wearing a dress that showed him a very nice pair of legs to go with everything else he admired.

He stood up and started towards her as she caught sight of him for the first time and her face lit up with a beaming smile. She came over hand outstretched. "So do I call you Nick or Inspector or what?"

He took her hand and held rather than shook it. "I thought we had sorted all that out, it's Nick and this is not official police business. I took the weekend off but I will want to ask you about Dan and the professor."

"Not all the time, I hope," she retorted with a smile, trying to extract her hand, she notice his embarrassment, "I'll need it for driving."

As they moved towards the door he asked, "So where we going… or is a secret?"

"It's somewhere nice, a village north of here. Hemingford Grey, have you ever heard of it?"

Now it was his turn to tease. "Can't say that I have, but there again unless it was the scene of a brutal murder it would never get into the police gazette."

She looked at him over the top of the car as she opened the door to get in. "If you feel like that perhaps we should have gone on a murder weekend."

"A sort of busman's holiday, you mean." "Damn it Inspector! Don't you ever relax?"

He smiled across at her. "I was kind of joking you know, but in answer to your question no... not in a long time... I think I must have got out of the habit."

"Well, let's see if we can do something about that. I think you'll like this place, great food and real ale, if you're into that sort of thing."

"Sounds just like my sort of place. Drive on my good woman, I deliver myself into your hands."

As they drove she asked, "So do you want to get the shop talk over while we drive or leave it until later?"

"I wasn't thinking along those lines at all. Like I said this isn't official police business. All I'm trying to understand is what would drive a person like Dan Davies to commit murder... and why that particular person? There must be a logical reason but I'm damned if I can see it. That aside I was hoping you might tell me something about yourself, what is you do, sounds awfully mysterious."

She laughed. "Nothing mysterious about it, I was going to give you a guided tour tomorrow, not that there is much to see. And if he's up to it we are having lunch with the professor on Sunday. He can fill in any blanks."

"Sounds marvellous, but are you sure I'm not screwing up your weekend entirely? I mean, if there is something else..?"

"If you don't want my company all you have to do is say, you know?"

"On the contrary, I've looked forward to this all week! It's just that I don't want you to feel you have to take care of the old fool all the time."

"There you go again with the apologies! And less of the old fool, please. You're not that much older than me and besides as you get to know me a little better, you'll realize I don't do what I don't want to do, OK?"

"Yes Ma'am, I like the sound of that."

"Like the sound of what?"

"The getting to know you better bit."

She turned that green eyed gaze upon him and smiled and in that second they both relaxed.

The Cock pub, at Hemingford Grey, was everything she had promised. Open fires, good English ale and fantastic food. But above all else, throughout the evening they relaxed more in each other's company. They compared notes on their individual lives, the ups and downs trials and successes. For instance, he discovered that as a student she had very nearly dropped out and if it hadn't been for the good professor she may well have done so. She touched on some of the early work she had done for the professor, including the interviews with Dan all those years ago.

But all too soon the pub landlord was calling time and it was over. Of course there was still the drive back to the hotel and there was always tomorrow and the next day as well.

His half jocular invitation for a night cap was politely declined, as part of the evening they both discovered that neither of them were great drinkers. With his sincere thanks for a very pleasant evening he closed the car door with a parting... "till tomorrow."

"I'll pick you up about ten thirty, if that's OK?" He waved his hand in acknowledgement, and she drove away he watched the taillights of her car down the road until she turned the corner and was gone.

The following morning he was up, showered breakfasted, and half way through the second newspaper. Why ten thirty, he thought as he checked his watch again, why not nine thirty or ten? I haven't anything else to do... Why should she? After all it was his weekend.

By way of some sort of unspoken compromise she arrived at a little past ten fifteen and found him in the lounge drinking coffee.

He stood up to greet her. "Are we in a hurry or have you time for coffee?"

She didn't even look at her watch. "We have all day. No timetable, no script to follow. Coffee sounds wonderful. So how did you sleep?"

"Like a baby, I can't remember the last time I felt so relaxed."

"An evening at the Cock has that effect on most people from out of town."

"I think the company may have had a fair bit to do with it as well."

"Why thank you, kind sir, we aim to please! After coffee, I thought we might go and take a look round the laboratories. As I said last night there's not a lot to see; you need the people to see what we really do."

"So tell me, you, the professor and these people get up to what exactly?"

"Wow! Where do I start?"

"The idiot version, if you please."

"Ah! That actually makes it harder, but if you insist," she laughed.

"You have obviously heard of prehistoric man, the tribes of North America the Aborigines of Australia? Well, if you study their folklore and customs you would discover the hierarchy or the structure of their civilization. In all of these cultures there were, and up to a point still are, the elders or wise men that rule but there was another, the Shaman or spiritual leader. He was very special. All communities had one, but the best and most successful groups centred on the most powerful Shaman."

"You mean spiritual, like a priest or church vicar?"

"No, not exactly, these people pre date the church and religion by thousands of years. In this context the Shaman was the link between this world and what they described as the spiritual world. Some were more healer than leader, but some had powers beyond comprehension, even by our present day powers of analysis. Some mythical beings, like Merlin the magician, were probably Shaman. We may even find out, one day, that Merlin was not a person but a title. Many of them used herbs and potions and hallucinogenic concoctions to great effect. They could spiritually leave their body on searching quests, to seek out game herds for the hunters."

Coffee over, they moved to the car and were on their way to the university where she worked as the story continued.

"Even today, in remote areas like Tibet, deep within the Amazon jungle, some of the more remote tribes of Africa, Australia and America, there are some who still have the art. You'll see. What the professor started and hopefully I will continue is that we believe these powers are not lost. Man has merely moved on but not necessarily in a good way. Religion and the church have much to answer for with their one God theory and death to all non believers…"

"Ok, but surely that was centuries ago?"

"That's when these powers were lost. The church was very powerful in those days, look how long it took them to admit that the heavens didn't revolve around the Earth.

Take the zealots of the Spanish Inquisition it was a very brave man who stood against the established church in those days. Then there's the attitude of the first settlers of North America to the natives they found there, just because they were half naked and worshipped the sun. The Spanish Conquistadors in South America, the missionaries in Africa, us again in Australia and New Zealand. We called them naked savages or heathens and because they couldn't speak our language or worship our God they were some how less than human."

He said, "I must admit I had never quite thought of it in that sort of way before. It was our history… it was the progress of civilization."

"But whose civilization… who said they were not civilized in their own right?"

"Ok, but surely that's all behind us, isn't it?"

"You wish! There is still tons of persecution in this world. Look at Communist China's attitude to Tibet, the Buddhists and the Dalai Lama. Christian versus Muslim and that's before you get into the real fruit loops of White Supremacists, religious fanatics and extremists."

"Point taken."

"Ours are still the laws of the jungle, might over right and the strong will always conquer the weak. Look at people like Stephen Hawking. How do you fancy your chances in a fight with him?"

"Physically no contest, but you mean against him, I'm a mental midget."

"Imagine where mankind would be if each new generation moved only forward from the previous generation. If only we took the best from each of us."

"Ok, fine, it's a great loss to mankind that we've seemingly lost a great talent. But surely that's in the very nature of evolutionary progress? I believe we once had gills and webs between our toes. But this is all academic theory and speculation, right?"

She smiled at him like a parent over an ignorant child. "No, it isn't. That power is within us all, that's what I've been trying to explain. We as a species have a very large brain over which we can control less than ten percent. The automatic side of our brain power, that tells you when to breathe, eat and sleep. The bit that stops us doing dumb things like lifting too heavy an object probably uses another ten twenty percent, so what about the rest of that capacity?"

"The professor had us looking at a phenomenon; let's call it out of body experiences. Dan was one of the subjects. Where someone who is close to death feels as though they have left their body and are floating around looking down at what is happening. Now because of those studies we concluded that there were just too many of them to ignore. The stories they told and the facts they revealed were way beyond anything that they could have witnessed any other way."

"Dan for instance, he was a brilliant subject. He had an almost clinical power of observation. The story he told us of seeing his own body being tended to by his sergeant and then watching the getaway car hit the other man and get away. Now if you think about that, even with the most sceptical mind, there is no way he could have witnessed any of that in a normal way. He had to have been outside his body."

As far as Nick was concerned she was not telling him anything he didn't already know, but it was fascinating none the less. You certainly couldn't doubt her commitment.

By this time they were in the car park and she was now giving him her full on concentration as she continued. "Now, all of the occurrences we recorded usually followed a traumatic experience, predictably a near fatal accident, but not always. The professor hypothesised what it would take to achieve the same effect without the traumatic trigger."

He was looking at her in a completely new light. This was not the bubbly girl of last night; she was now in full scientific doctor mode. Her face was serious, her breathing shallow, as she hammered home point after point, looking at him to make sure he was taking it all in.

Their eyes met and instinctively he reached out and took her hand as he said, "My God, you're not theorising any more, are you? You've actually done it! There are people here that can actually leave their bodies at will."

She let her breath go in a rush, and her face lit up with her most brilliant smile and just like professor Henry Higgins she said, "By George, he's got it! That and a whole lot more. Come on let's go and see."

The little girl was back. She took his hand and led him across the car park, past security and into her secret world. As he expected the place was half in darkness and deserted. She disappeared for a second and the whole place lit up. It was... different. He hadn't the faintest clue of what he had expected but this... The room was made up of many cubicles and they looked solid and a little bit sinister. Some had a small table and chair while others had a cot. All seemed to have thick light, deadening curtains and heavy doors. There were a lot of electronic gizmo tape recorders, video recorders, playback machines, CCTV cameras and things he could only guess at everywhere.

"Impressed?"

She came back towards him, hands behind her back with a strange girlish skip in her step that said that she would be very disappointed if he wasn't.

"Yes, very. It's not what I expected when you said laboratory, though. I don't know, there's not a Petri dish or a Bunsen burner in sight."

"You were expecting odd body bits, all stitched together with wires dangling."

"Not exactly, it's not how I pictured you working with the minds of people, that's all."

"We have a full medical staff here as well. Doctors, psychiatrist's all sorts. Would you like to see some videos?"

They wandered over to a small seating area that housed a wide screen TV. "There's a sort of coffee machine in the corridor. It's not brilliant, but it's wet and warm."

"No thanks, I get enough bad coffee at work we have to send out for anything decent. Really, I can hold out until lunchtime."

She fiddled with a tape and stood up with the remote in her hand. "This one is a woman, one of our stars. The man you will see is someone just off the street we asked to help with the experiment."

They watched, as the blue screen flickered and focused as a woman, Nick guessed in her mid thirties, came into view. To him she didn't look particularly special. The woman was led into one of the cubicles behind them. A white-coated girl accompanied her and as the woman lay down on the cot the girl started to attach wires.

"We monitor all heart and brain activity for any signs of trouble. The procedure is not painful, nor is there any special preparation or drug inducement."

Once the girl was finished, a disembodied voice said, tape rolling, monitoring all vital signs. The girl came over to the window and drew a blind and closed the thick curtains. She switched the main light out and closed the door. There was obviously still a source of light in the room, because Nick could see the woman as clear as day as she lay motionless. At this point the TV picture split to show two screens; each screen had the date and time counters running in synchronisation to show there had been no post editing.

"You can concentrate your viewing on the man. There really is nothing to see as far as the woman is concerned, she just lies there as you see her throughout the entire experiment."

Nick focused on the man who was seated at a table in another cubicle. In front of him were three black plastic envelopes, identical in every way except they had large white numbers on them: 1, 2, and 3. In front of the bags were three plain white pieces of card or paper and they too were marked, but with letters A, B, and C. Finally there was a small note pad and a smaller black envelope.

A voice, that Nick recognised as Alan Redman said from behind the camera, "When I leave the room I want you to draw three different objects of your own choosing. Keep them simple but recognisable. When you have done that I want you to repeat the drawings in the small note pad. Then place the drawings one in each envelope, in any order you choose. Write your choices down in the note book, A1, B2 or whatever against each of the images. Finally, seal all the envelopes, including the one with the note book, then press the red button on the wall by the door and the exercise will be complete. Do you understand?"

The man nodded.

"Do you have any questions?"

The man shook his head.

"Very well, I will close this blind and draw the curtains to ensure there can be no outside influence upon your choices of image. There is no time limit to the exercise.

You can take as much or as little time as you want. If at any time you wish to stop the exercise, all you have to do is to press the red button and the exercise will be terminated. Do you understand?"

Again Nick watched as the man nodded. He heard the noises of the blind being pulled, the curtains being drawn and the door closing.

To his amazement the TV screen divided into four; a CCTV image of the closed doors and curtained windows was also displayed. "You're very meticulous, I'll give you that."

"We have to be, if we are ever to be taken seriously in our work. There can be no room for ambiguity or any possibility of accusations of trickery or false claims."

The man in the room just sat there for a few minutes, gathering his thoughts Nick supposed. Then he picked up the large felt tipped pen and started drawing. The camera angle was all wrong Nick couldn't see what the man was drawing.

"I can't see what he's doing."

"You're not supposed to, not at this stage. If anybody on the outside could see what he is doing we could open ourselves up to accusations of tampering. He will do three drawings and place them in envelopes and seal them, unobserved except by the camera you are watching, which is there to ensure no-one enters the room during the experiment. If this were a really important experiment we would bring in official adjudicators to double check and monitor every step of the procedure as well."

While they were talking the man appeared to finish his task. He rose and crossed the room. Nick heard a buzzer sound and a light flashing off camera. The door was opened almost immediately and Alan Redman came back and took the man away. The envelopes remained in full view of the camera which kept recording.

Jill said, "The man's task is complete. You can turn your attention back to the woman on the cot."

Nick sat there in stunned silence. After a few minutes he could hear the woman breathing, shallow at first, like someone asleep, but the rhythm was breaking, she was waking up. Slowly the woman opened her eyes and sat up. To him she looked a little dazed and disorientated but that seemed to pass. She reached under the pillow on the bed and produced a note pad and an envelope, this one was white. For a few minutes the woman sat there on the cot filling in the note pad then she closed the pad, put it in the envelope and sealed it. She rose from the bed, leaving the white envelope in full view, and moved towards the door where she pressed a button and waited. Soon she was led away.

His attention glued to the big screen, Nick watched as Alan Redman and Jilly each went into a cubicle. The camera's recording as they went; one picked up the single white envelope while the other retrieved the black ones. The screen returned to two pictures, one on each of them as they approached a central point under the view of yet another camera.

Sitting at the table was none other than the good professor. The camera watched as he took the white envelope and opened it. The camera zoomed in on the contents which showed almost child like drawings of three images.

Jilly said, "She's no artist but good enough."

Nick could clearly see three distinctly different images; what looked to be a house drawn by a child, rectangular with four windows, a door right in the middle and a pointed roof with a chimney at each side. Next to the drawing she had written A3. The second image was a reasonably well drawn cube with the writing B1 next to it, and finally a tree with C2 written by it.

The professor with due ceremony carefully opened the black envelopes one by one, making certain to place the contents on top of the envelope before moving to the next.

Envelope 1 produced the card with a large letter B on it and a picture of a well drawn cube shape. Envelope 2 had the exact same tree shape and the letter C. And it came as no surprise when envelope 3 contained card A and a childish picture of a house.

"That is truly amazing, how in God's name did she do that? Are we talking ESP here or something?"

"Nowhere near... we have tried looking at ESP but it's a far too hit and miss affair, little more than prediction really, the success rate was very poor. As you can see Gladys achieved one hundred percent accuracy."

"This isn't like stage magic, is it? Where you show me the trick but won't tell me how it's done."

She laughed. "It's not magic. You have just witnessed an experiment involving a controlled out of body experience."

"You mean…"

"Yep! She cheated. She was in the room with that man, looking over his shoulder as he took part in the experiment. She can do it at will."

"That's unbelievable, I can't imagine…"

"Dan was another one who could do it at will. We were trying experiments over distances to see how far he could get away from his body."

"But… isn't that a bit risky… dangerous even?"

"That's it, we just don't know. Allegedly the seekers, the Shaman of old could travel miles in search of the herds they would hunt, but of course that's hearsay. I'll be perfectly honest with you, there is a high element of risk in what we are doing here, if a link were ever broken…. Of course, other experiments we do here involving telekinesis and levitation are nowhere near as risky."

"Tele what?"

"Telekinesis, it's the effecting of movement without physical contact, using the power of the mind to move objects. We have one guy we call the Poltergeist, he can literally destroy a room, just by thinking about it."

"But I thought… aren't Poltergeist just ghosts or something?"

"Noisy mischievous spirit, I think that's the literal translation. It's German. That's what everybody thought, but we think it has a more human origin. In the past whenever a poltergeist phenomenon was encountered, it was assumed that a house or a person was being haunted. However, more recent thinking has theorised that it may in fact be a real person who is using telekinetic power, most likely subconsciously, to raise havoc, or punish someone close to them. It may even be a cry for help."

"Please, Miss! I need some coffee, real stuff! You're turning my very rational world upside down, I hope you realise that."

She smiled as she shut down the TV and put the video back in its box and back under lock and key. "Consider yourself lucky that it's me giving the tour! Now if it were professor Harman-Jones, he really would make your eyeballs rotate. He is almost fanatical about the subject and can talk for hours on it, it's his life."

"I'll bear that in mind when we meet. I'll keep the conversation on loose cars and fast women, or should that be the other way around?"

"Is that your area of expertise, Inspector?"

"One of many, although current experiences of either are few and far between."

"Sorry to disappoint you, but I am neither fast nor loose. In all respects I like to take my time and enjoy the experience, it's much more fun"

Nick was in awe of this woman OK he admitted to himself that he was well out of practise when it came to dealing with the opposite sex these days. But as gently as possible he was probing, testing to see how far he could go. However she had his measure, he was flirting with her and she was flirting right back at him. She was giving as good as she got, and perhaps better.

They left the car in the car park and walked to where they could get him his brain reviving coffee.

"Questions?" she asked.

He took a long pull at his coffee. "One of these may not be sufficient. I had no idea that anything like that was going on, or for that matter was even possible. Is there much of this kind of research going on? Is it commonplace for people to be floating around like that?"

"There are studies going on all over the world. If we're successful we may even be allowed to enter a couple of special events in the Olympics, fifty metre levitation race or the telekinetic javelin."

"You are joking, aren't you?"

The little girl was back, teasing him and poking fun at his ignorance.

"Just a little, but it is all very hush, hush. We don't exactly exchange notes or anything. Everything is a closely guarded secret and I must ask you to respect that.

Everything you saw this morning is classified secret. You can imagine what would happen if the press ever got hold of it."

"I understand, your secrets are safe with me. I'm grateful you're taking the time to explain all this to me, it's helping, I think."

"As to your question of people floating about all over the place, as flippant as it was intended, the simple answer is we don't know. There is absolutely no way of knowing. When it happens, how it happens or where it happens there is no way to detect their presence."

"Wow! Now that is a frightening prospect."

"Yes, yes it is! Hence the need for secrecy, although we are fairly certain that there are military versions of our experiments going on, again probably all over the world."

"The ultimate in Big Brother technology, now that is scary."

"So what would you like to do now? We can go back to the lab and watch more tapes..."

"Pass! I think I have more knowledge than is good for a layman, don't you think?"

"Pity, I was hoping you would like to learn more, maybe even learn how to do it for yourself."

"Are you kidding? Laying alone in a darkened room on a bed made for one, is not my idea of a pleasant way to pass a Saturday afternoon, if it's all the same to you."

"I shudder to think what you might say if I asked what your ideal way of spending a quiet Saturday afternoon would entail."

There it was again, he pushed and she pushed back, no horrified or shocked rejection, just a veiled hint.

"You could show me around Cambridge."

"Now that I can do, follow me," and she took off up the road and down to the river. "There is only one way to see Cambridge and that is by punt. Do you want to drive or will you wimp out and let me?"

"Aren't there any water taxis around, then we could both wimp out, as you so delicately put it?"

She laughed that laugh and instantly became that little girl again, he could fall in love with this woman, it would be so easy.

"You take me so seriously, Inspector. I was only joking about making either of us drive. That water is far too cold at this time of year for either of us to get stuck up a pole as the punt drifts serenely away. Besides, leave it to the professional, that's what I always say."

As the afternoon passed towards evening his thoughts turned to dinner. "I hope you're not busy tonight? I was hoping I could take you to dinner."

"Already taken care of... How do you like your steak cooked?"

"That's easy, burnt black on the outside and red raw in the middle."

"Hey! There's a coincidence! That's more or less how I cook 'em."

"Are you sure? Surely after working all day wouldn't you rather eat out?"

"Most people only say that when I offer to cook the second time."

He looked into those eyes. "I'm a working bachelor you know, I have the constitution of an ox, and I accept your kind offer, provided you allow me to return the favour at my place some time."

"That's what I like in a man, the threat of retaliation before the first blow is struck. To the kitchen, and may the worst cook win."

As with many things that day she had not been entirely serious about her abilities in the kitchen. The meal was perfect, right down to the candlelight and the soft music playing quietly in the background. The room was pleasantly warm from a gas log effect fire burning in the grate. From the large cushions scattered on the floor near the fire this was obviously a favourite spot to relax and Nick took full advantage of it. When she returned from the kitchen she came and stood over him and he looked up at her with sleepy eyes.

"If you're trying to get rid of me, I have to warn you that you are going completely the wrong way about it. I just thought you should know."

She sank to her knees close to him. "How do you know it's not a trap?"

"Oh I do hope so, I'm tired of sparring with you. You're too good at it! I'm so out of practise with this whole he/she business, all that sexual harassment political correctness mumbo jumbo. Life was so much easier in my day when you just clubbed the women over the head and dragged them back by the hair to your cave."

"Then let me spell it out for you," and as she spoke her soft hair fell across his face and their lips met. They kissed twice more before she stretched full length beside him.

He said, "I was just going to start the washing up…"

"You can do it later."

"I was joking."

"I wasn't," she said as she kissed him again.

Sunday was a lazy affair, they got up late, but Nick decided that he had better make tracks to the hotel. He needed to shave and change before lunch with the professor. She said, "It won't be a long lunch, he really isn't up to it these days. But he wants to see you, set your mind at rest, if he can."

"Hell, I don't know what to think any more. I am as confused now as I ever hope to be, some detective. Huh!" He found it strange but she said nothing. It was time to change tack. He came over to her and took her hand. "About last night, please tell me that it meant as much to you as it did for me."

She smiled weakly at him. "I have no regrets, if that's what you mean."

"Will you stop with the teasing? I don't…Didn't believe in love at first sight but…"

She put a finger to his lips. "Its early days, don't spoil it. I'm not teasing you, I really don't know what I feel right now, is that love? I don't know... I mean I love the professor but that's not the same thing, is it? I love my work and I have always shunned any distractions. Perhaps I have kidded myself into believing that I'm in total control of every situation and that I was in charge of this one too."

He looked at her and saw gentle tears flowing down her cheeks.

"Do you want me to go?"

"Damn you!" She slammed a fist into his shoulder. "Will you stop being so...so bloody gentlemanly! Call me a whore...a slut... or treat me like an easy lay, hit me if you want to but don't love me."

She sank to her knees and wept into his lap.

"Too late," he whispered, "and I have no intentions of calling you any of those things. If it was a mistake then so be it, I'll just go. You can make my apologies to the professor when you see him and we'll leave it like that. What is it they say, there's no fool like an old fool, is there?"

Her fist caught him again. "Stop it! Stop it! You can't love me, you don't even know me. I never meant... Oh Christ, I'm so sorry."

"Look you're not making any sense. I don't want to leave you like this, help me understand."

She got up from the floor tear streaming down her face she started to run towards the bedroom. "Just go, get the hell away from me, and leave me alone." And with that the bedroom door slammed shut against him.

Nick picked up his jacket and left. "Bloody women, I'll never understand them, if I live to be a hundred!" he muttered, and slammed her front door as he left.

Still fuming, he reached the hotel and checked out immediately to go home. But all the way back he couldn't get her out of his mind, what had he done wrong? Had he pushed too far too quickly? But how could that be? He had flirted and teased her but she had made the opening moves, her place for dinner... the first kiss. He slammed his fist so hard into the empty seat beside him it made dust rise and an old woman two rows down the isle of the carriage looked up and gave him a strange look.

When he reached his flat, he tore off his clothes and headed for the shower to wash her sweet scent from him, blast the ache from his shoulders write her off as just a pleasant distraction... his one and only one night stand.

Chapter 6

The following day back in familiar surroundings, he ignored all requests for information about his weekend. He smiled and dodged the questions with hints and innuendo to satisfy his colleague's morbid curiosity and to avoid any admission that it had been an unmitigated disaster.

In the comfort of his own office he pulled out his private note book and added notes from his weekend experience. He reviewed the notes along with everything else he had pieced together. And with a sigh he slammed it shut, thinking that he still didn't know a damn thing. At the end of the day he was not one bloody step closer to the truth, whatever the hell that might be.

Reluctantly he thought of Jilly Tindell. If he was honest with himself he couldn't get her out of his mind, he was besotted with her. But he was also totally confused by the whole affair He smiled to himself, affair, that's a laugh! What was wrong with her? Was it her work? Was he such a distraction? She had willingly submitted to his fumbling advances, but then had she immediately regretted the move? But why, what was so terribly wrong with him?

He tried to push her from his mind, at least the romantic thoughts of her. He tried desperately to concentrate on the scientific content of the weekend. He had learnt a lot and it had all been fascinating stuff, but so what? She had offered to answer his questions, fill in gaps about Dan Davies… but had she?

OK, Dan had had an out of body experience around the time he had been shot. He had met the professor, become a student of sorts. Because of that Dan could leave his body at will and become a searcher, so what?

It was all academic research, yes? He could understand the significance of the research and some of the more frightening prospects. If and when they had perfected the technique but there again, surely the opposition and other countries were doing pretty much the same thing.

Suddenly a thought occurred to him and he picked up the phone and dialled.

"Professor Harman-Jones's department, Alan Redman speaking. How can I help?"

"Alan, it's Nick Burton again. Listen I'm sorry to be a bloody nuisance, but could I ask a question?"

"Course you can. Do you want me to get Jilly or the professor?"

"No, please don't disturb them. It's not that important and I'm sure you will know the answer. Has there ever been any documented incident of a person supposedly leaving their body and entering another?"

There was total silence from the other end of the line.

"Alan?"

"Sorry Inspector, you caught me unawares there. Made me think a bit, but no, as far as I can recollect that is not something I've ever heard of. But I can check with the others if you like and get back to you."

"No, no it's not that important, I'm happy with your answer, thanks."

"Can I ask what prompted the question, Inspector?"

"I don't know really, just sitting here trying to make sense of everything I learnt over the weekend. It was quite a crash course, if you know what I mean. Look, I'm sorry to have disturbed you, just forget it. I'm sure it's just me getting everything wrapped round my neck. Thanks for your time," and he hung up.

One other benefit he had acquired from the weekend was the taste of real food again. It had occurred to him that over the past few months, alright years, he had become lazy and let himself go. He had become far too dependant on the take-away restaurants or the frying pan if he bothered to cook at all. Unfortunately, this train of thought led right back to women or one woman in particular. He shook his head and headed for the door. He thought he would visit the supermarket on his way home and treat himself to some decent ingredients for a change. He would forget all this Dan Davies nonsense for the night and just watch a movie or something.

In his tiny kitchenette he was having fun and enjoying himself preparing a one man feast when the door bell rang. Bugger! He thought, probably Miss Finch with another mysterious envelope. Well to hell with the lot of them! If it is, then it can damn well wait until tomorrow.

He snatched the door open and he was ready with 'I've got something on the cooker speech...' as he looked straight into a pair of dazzling green eyes. Although he admitted to himself that these eyes seemed to have lost some of their sparkle... and could he detect the hint of redness around them.

"You! Well, I'll be damned."

"You and me both probably," she replied, "Can we talk?"

He stood back and let her in closing the door behind her. "Talk away, although I would have thought you'd made your feelings perfectly clear yesterday. But be my guest."

"You called the lab this morning, I thought you might have wanted to talk to me, and chickened out when Alan answered the phone and asked the first thing that came into your head."

She's fishing, he thought.

"You came all this way just for that? Nice try missy, but I think you'd better try again."

"Look I hurt you, I'm sorry. I shouldn't have got that involved, that wasn't part…"

"Of the plan," he finished her sentence for her. You can drop the act, he thought.

"Is this about you and me…or what? Or is it about your precious bloody professor and your sodding work. Something has gone wrong… something has happened that scares the hell out of all of you. And then along comes PC Plod with his big boots stomping through the whole thing and you were sent to head me off at the pass."

"I…I don't know what you're talking about…it's…"

"I thought I told you to drop the act, its over. Plod has finally worked it out, or at least most of it. You were supposed to be a diversion, find out what I knew… give me all the cooperation in the world and tell me nothing. I don't know if sex was any part of the plan? I just hope it was as good for you as it was for me. Was that it? Poor old soul… over the hill hasn't had a bit in a while… feel sorry for me, did you?"

Tears were streaming down her face and her whole body was shaking. He wanted to go to her, take her up in his arms, kiss away the tears and tell her how much he loved her. But she had used him, tried to fool him and divert his attention away from the truth.

"It wasn't like that! Yes, I was supposed to get close to you and find out what you knew, but that was all. I liked Dan, we all did but what we are doing is far too important to be jeopardised by personal issues."

"Is that what I am, a personal issue?"

"Yes!... No!... Hell, I don't know. I didn't intend to fall in love with you..."

"What did you say?" Now his confidence was waning.

"That's what I wanted to say to you yesterday but I couldn't. I had deliberately set out to deceive you... steer you away from us and the project... give you the tour, show you that there was no possible connection between Dan Davies and our work. Yes, even sleeping with you, if it would take your mind off the damn case of yours."

"So what went wrong?"

"You, you went wrong... you're a very easy person to like, Nick Burton. I was lying through my teeth, deceiving you and you treated me like a lady. I treated you like shit and you acted like a gentleman. I tried to warn you off by saying you didn't know who I was, and you still don't."

"I know enough, and yes I do love you, in spite of all this, that doesn't change."

"Damn you, there you go again." She rushed into his arms, her sobs rocking her body as he held her tight "How can you say you love me when..."

"Question is did you mean it when you said you love me?"

The answer was the faintest of whispers. "Oh y-e-s!"

"I suppose if this was the movies, then the volume of music would start to increase and I should sweep you off your feet and carry you away to the bedroom as the screen fades into darkness."

She pulled out of his arms. "So who or what's stopping you?"

He shrugged, "I'm hungry, how about you?"

"I haven't eaten a thing since yesterday."

"Then I suggest you go and freshen up and I'll finish cooking dinner."

Nearly twenty minutes he walked over to the bedroom door. "BONG! Dinner is served, me lady."

A lazy voice answered, "Do I have to dress for dinner?"

"Not if you don't want to, but I should warn you if you intend to dine naked I may drool a lot."

She came out of his bedroom, dressed in his dressing gown, which was a mile too big for her. "Then I shall wear this."

He burst out laughing at the sight. "How gallant you are, sir! If you want to practise your drooling, just imagine what I'm wearing underneath."

"Will you be serious? I'm trying to remember I'm still hungry and that I have slaved away in a moderately warm kitchen for, well at least twenty-five minutes?"

"OK, let's eat but dessert might have to wait."

"And what desert might that be?"

They lay silently in the darkened room, locked in each others arms when finally she asked, "So who or what gave me away, Sherlock?"

"You did, all by yourself. This morning, I went fishing, I threw a hook with a big fat worm on the end into the pond and low and behold look what I caught," and he gave her a gentle squeeze.

"I don't understand, I came here to…"

"Shh! don't say any more, didn't you hear me say I'd worked it out for myself? This morning was to test my theory. I played the dumb cop asking dumb questions but Alan wasn't at all convinced, was he? Who did he run to, you or the professor? Not that it matters much either way, what I asked was serious enough to scare the hell out of you all. Whose idea was it for you to come here today? That took some guts after yesterday's performance."

He could feel her stiffen under his arm. "So just how did I give myself away?"

"In the end lots of ways, but it started yesterday with your reaction to the previous night's activity that clearly hadn't been in the script. What you said and how you said it didn't make any sense. I couldn't believe, or more to the point my ego wouldn't let me believe, I had misread your signals so badly. Yet there you were calling yourself a whore, and all sorts of other ugly things? Yeah! I was upset and mad as hell at you, but I kept asking myself, why the sudden change of heart?"

"Then when I finally calmed down and started to think with my brains again, things started to pop into place. Turning up at the funeral, why would you bother? With the professor's health problems a wreath would have been enough, hell nobody outside Cambridge even knew about the connection between you! You wouldn't have been missed. No, that had to be for my benefit, where else would we ever meet so conveniently by chance? You had to find out how much I knew, or thought I knew, and the only logical reason for thinking along those lines was that something had gone badly wrong. During your experiments, or whatever, Dan had said or done something to start the alarm bells going before he died. Had he passed that information on to someone else, me perhaps?"

"The video tapes, Dan's last farewell speech and the one about his near death experiences... they were recorded on the equipment at your lab. Now, that really was a silly mistake. All done to convince me there was nothing to find out. The delivery by hand, was that because you thought I was making too much progress? Who was the courier, you or Allan?"

Her answer came out as a croak. "It was Alan, he was just supposed to pop in and leave them. It was your nosey old neighbour, she stuck her head out and saw him the second time, so he pretended to be a courier and got her to sign for the package."

"Nice touch that, but if you really knew how little I actually know then you wouldn't have bothered, and I would still be bumbling around in the dark."

"Then the invitation and the guided tour, so generous so personal, cleverly structured to reveal all and divulge nothing. Look! Dan was here but what he did recently is nothing to do with us, honest."

"However, what Dan did, and for whatever reason he did it, attracted the attention of the press and the other media and that couldn't be allowed. That's what this has been about all along, protecting the project from the media. All the time feeding me all that stuff to muddy the waters."

"Then finally, I ask a policeman's dumb question and low and behold you're sent charging in to find out if I'm really onto something or what? Of course the fact that it's you who came confirms that what happened Saturday night was not part of the overall plan. Obviously, you haven't told them about it or they would never have let you come, would they?"

"No," said in a whisper, which was all the response she could muster.

"Yet here you are, turning up at my home address! How on earth did you know where I lived? I'm not in Who's Who, or the telephone directory. I never told you and it's certainly not something you could have learnt from my police station. So again, it had to have been Dan. How am I doing?"

When she spoke it was in a tense course whisper. "We'd make pretty lousy criminals, wouldn't we?"

"I certainly wouldn't recommend a change of profession, at least not on my patch."

She went on, "One bit I don't understand. You said we were feeding you all that stuff. What stuff? We only sent you the two tapes Dan made he said it might help if you got too nosey."

Now it was his turn to go rigid, what did that mean? Was she admitting to everything he was accusing her of, except, she wasn't.... Did that mean there was still someone else involved... was there still a Mr. X?

"So, what will happen now? Are you going to arrest me?" She asked with more concern in her voice than she intended.

"If I did you'd probably get life."

"Life!" It was practically a scream.

"What's wrong with that? Would life with me be so bad?"

"Life with you?... What the hell are you talking about?"

"Marriage of course, it would be the only way you could secure my undying loyalty to your cause and prevent me from revealing all I know. Besides a husband can't be made to testify against his wife, and so far I'm the only witness for the prosecution."

From somewhere in the dark and under the bed clothes she hit him hard. "Will you stop talking like a bloody policeman for one second and tell me again what you just said? Did you just ask me to marry you or something?"

"Or something."

"After everything I've put you through?"

"Yep!"

"You're mad!"

"Yep! So, will you do it?"

"Marry you just to keep you quiet?"

"I can't promise to keep quiet, so what do you say?"

"Yep!"

In the morning she said, "Christ, look at the time! I've got to get back to Cambridge I've got a lecture to give in two hours' time."

"I'd tidy myself up a bit first, if you go looking like that everybody will know what you were up to last night."

"Perhaps if you were more help, go and make some coffee or something. Have you got a hair brush …"

"But my interrogation isn't over yet."

"Oh, but it is Mister... I don't trust your techniques! Shouldn't there be another officer present? Or something like that I've seen the movies?"

"A threesome, is that what you mean, man or woman?"

"Now I know why they call you lot pigs! Anyway you said you'd worked it all out. What is there left you don't know?"

He went deadly serious. "I need to know what happened to make Dan flip."

She came over to him and put her arms around his neck and kissed him. "Can it wait until tonight? I really, really do have to be somewhere else right now."

"Then I suggest you let me go before I put you under very close arrest. Call me and I'll meet the train. We can go to a restaurant and you can fill me in with all the gory details. Tell the professor your secret is safe with me, who can I tell that would a) believe me or b) understand one single word. Remember I've been there and I'm not sure I believe it yet."

One more kiss and she was gone.

Morning prayers were cancelled that morning. Everyone was out at the scene of a crime that had happened during the early hours. Together with DC Martin, DC Riley and the SOCO team, they were reviewing the known facts. To them it was obviously another incident involving the Stringer family, it didn't really matter which one, they would all have cast iron alibis and a thousand witnesses. It had been a pretty vicious attack on a couple of black youths. Mary Riley asked, "Racist attack do you think?"

Nick took a look around and at some of the digital photographs that had been taken when his people had first arrived and before the victims had been taken to hospital.

"No, the Stringers are not racist... Well I'm sure they are racists as well as a number of other things. What I mean is they wouldn't smash someone's kneecaps just because they were black, there's no profit in it. Turf war would be my guess."

Sergeant Martin snorted, "Who'd be dumb enough to make a move onto the Stringers patch?"

Nick replied, "Take Mary, go to the hospital and ask them that very question. Stop by the station and pick up the travel version of the rouges gallery, see if they can identify anybody. Hell who knows, if they're dumb enough to move in on the Stringers they may be dumb enough to testify against them as well."

As he was taking a final look around the crime scene his cell phone rang. He looked at the screen. All it said was HQ, he punched the button and spoke, "DCI Burton."

A polite and efficient voice at the other end said, "please hold for DCC Hardcastle," Nick did as he was told.

He didn't have to wait long before the familiar gruff voice spoke in his ear, "Burton, what are you doing right now?"

"Just finishing off at the scene of last night's attack on two black youths…" He wasn't allowed to finish his sentence.

"Good, good, bring what you know to my office right away will you? It's just possible there's a link. Was it a racist attack, do you think?"

"I don't think so Sir it has all the hallmarks of a Stringer family punishment beating, kneecap job."

"Stringers you say, good… good, get here as quick as you can. I'm calling a meeting, need you here" and the line went dead before he could answer.

He looked puzzled at the tiny phone in his hand, what the hell was that about? He got a lift to police HQ in the area car that was at the scene, but before he went inside he called DS Martin and got DC Mary Riley instead.

"Martin, either someone's kicked you very hard or I've got the wrong number."

"It's Riley, sir. DS Martin's still arguing with the doctors at the moment."

"Have you anything of any use for me on that front?" He asked her.

"DS Martin's getting them put into a private ward on an upper floor with a uniform guard on the door. Needless to say we are not getting too much cooperation or answers to our questions. Suddenly they've gone all Jamaican and no 'Speakie Inglish' on us. Although when I threatened to hand them over to immigration the eyes got awful big."

"What do you reckon, Yardies?"

"That's our guess at the moment ,sir."

"Good work! Tell Dave that if he gets any static from uniform about the guard, refer them to the DCC. I'm on my way there now."

There was a message waiting for him at the reception desk to go to the small conference room upon arrival. He found the room he was looking for and tried to enter as quietly as possible, not to distract the speaker or draw any unnecessary attention to himself. Unfortunately he didn't take into account DCC Hardcastle sitting at the head of the table.

"Burton, glad you could make it. Now we can get on with things."

Nick felt the colour on his cheeks, like a naughty schoolboy late for class. As he reached a seat he glanced around the table at his fellow attendees, who were just a sea of unidentified faces. But he did recognise the fact that he was certainly in august company. Of the uniformed representatives he didn't see anyone lower than Chief Inspector. As far as those in plain clothes he hadn't a clue who they were, or where they were from. He guessed Drug Squad, Special Branch, maybe even Customs. He resolved that after the meeting he would go along to the DCC's secretary and get a list of Who's Who. However, the one thing that was blatantly obvious to him from this gathering was that Hardcastle was making it an all outsider event. With the exception of the DCC and himself there was no one else from their own division. He had long since suspected that the Stringers had an informant within the local force. Now it seemed that the DCC shared the same concern.

Hardcastle was through the preliminaries and just getting into his stride. "We've had a bit of intelligence that there's some major action brewing in our area. Needless to say it involves our local organised crime family… the Stringers and some outsiders who are trying to takeover some of their business, namely the supply of drugs. These new comers are of Jamaican origin and several groups seem to have moved into this area quite recently. I think the general term for these people is 'Yardies.'" He looked around the table for approval and saw a sea of nodding heads. He continued, "Unlike our home grown villainy they have an eager willingness to use extreme force against any and all who cross them."

"It goes without saying this is not good news, we do not want these people here, mixing in with our local thugs. According to the Met, Yardies prefer to use firearms as a first rather than a last resort and the last thing we need is gun warfare on our streets."

"We also know from past experiences that the Stringers will not give an inch without a fight, and to all intents and purposes it has already started. We believe that the attack carried out on two black youths on an industrial estate at the edge of town last night was a warning shot from the Stringer family of their intentions." He looked at Nick. "Would you concur with that, Chief Inspector Burton?"

Nick cleared his throat, "Yes sir, the two youths were kneecapped and it has all the hallmarks of the Stringers handiwork. I can confirm that the two youths are of Jamaican origin and are not being particularly helpful to our enquiries. We have them isolated at the local general hospital and with your permission, Sir I would like to place a twenty-four guard on them."

With a nod Hardcastle continued, "Quite! Personally I wouldn't lose too much sleep if all the local low life was to eliminate each other, quietly and efficiently, but we know that won't be the case. It will, if we allow it, spill out on to the streets and innocent civilians will be at great risk. I don't intend for that to happen. Thanks to our inside resources we know what is going to happen next and more importantly where. From all of those gathered here I propose we launch a joint operation trap."

The room became a buzz of speculative mumbles and Nick could feel the intense inter departmental rivalry bubbling just below the surface. All the important little questions were there: Who would be in charge? Who would get the greater share of the credit, if it went right? Who would shoulder the blame if it all went wrong?

Hardcastle let them speculate while he himself took time to pour a glass of water and take a long drink.

He called the room back to order, "Gentlemen! In this instance time is of the essence. The Stringer family does not intend to let the grass grow under their feet, and neither will we. The Yardies have obviously made their opening move and the Stringers have responded. I can't imagine that it will be too long before the Yardies answer in kind. I anticipate at least one or possibly two bodies to turn up within the next twelve to twenty-four hours. For all our sakes, let us hope that the dead will be non members of the Stringer family and only minor players in their organisation. If our Jamaican friends chose to target the family direct and actually kill one of them then we can expect all out war before the week is out."

"As far as we know a message has been sent to the head of one of the Yardie groups, calling for a truce and a meeting. All the groups have been invited. Presumably the Stringers will want to put on a huge show of strength in an attempt to limit the Yardie activity within their territorial area. They will try and seek some trade off advantage to allowing them to stay, but it will be on Stringer family terms."

"We are here to draw up our counter strategy. Gentlemen, we have before us a grand opportunity to strike a huge blow for law enforcement. On this one occasion we will have two powerful groups of criminals in a tightly confined space. I intend that none shall escape through the net. Your job today is to make that strategy come true, any questions?"

"How long do we have, sir?"

Hardcastle looked at his watch. "A little over seven hours… Lunch has been ordered, nothing has a higher priority."

"That's hardly enough time to coordinate…"

"Sorry, but we are not setting the time frame here. We are just responding to it."

"Sir, who's going to be in charge and where will it be coordinated from?"

"I will assume overall command from here. DCI Burton there will be your local liaison. It's his area; he has first hand knowledge and experience of the Stringers and what resources we can muster from here. Anything else we need will have to come from and through the people in this room. I expect, and the Commissioner backs me on this, your fullest cooperation for this operation. Failure is not an option on this one, and I promise you screw this up and it won't just be the Stringers out looking for heads. Gentlemen…The clock is ticking."

The DCC left the platform and came over to Nick and clapped him solidly on the shoulder. "Well me boy, welcome to the deep end."

"Sir," Nick spluttered, "that is an understatement if ever there was one. I never had so much as a sniff that the Stringers were up to anything on this scale."

"Thought we at HQ did nothing all day except sit on our well padded backsides and go out on bashes at night, is that it?"

"No sir, but…"

"Only joking lad! We've been alerted to the Yardies moving in by the Met boys. Seems they like to keep tabs on them, damn tricky job by all accounts."

"You said you knew what and where, care to share that knowledge, they're bound to ask?"

"I'll tell you this much, but it's not to leave the room. The meeting, if it happens at all, will be out in the open in the local football stadium."

"Christ sir, I hope you're still joking! That place has got to have at least twenty, thirty exits. It's like a bloody rabbit warren inside, tunnels and passageways and the like."

Hardcastle smiled; "Exciting, what?"

"Not one of the words I would have used, given time to think about it."

"Anyway, over to you me boy... I've got to go and brief the brass hats. I'll be back about four."

As the DCC departed the room, as one they turned towards him and a wall of questions came at him in a wave. After about half an hour he got out of the room with a list of questions that needed answers and demands for information that he needed to supply. First he called for backup from his own troops, he needed more hands.

While he was wondering where he could get hold of the plans of the football stadium his phone rang. He didn't recognise the number calling but he answered it anyway, it was Jill.

"Is this a good time?"

"Actually," he said, "I was going to call you, about tonight. Can we postpone? I'm going to be working late."

"Coo! Is it something big?"

"I can't tell you but if all goes well I'm sure you'll read all about it in the morning papers."

Her tone changed immediately. "Sounds dangerous to me, you will be careful, won't you?"

"I'll call you when it's all over, how's that? So can we make dinner tomorrow instead of tonight?"

"Of course we can; but you ring me, and I don't care what time of day it is, promise me?"

"You're beginning to sound like a wife already."

"No joking around, I'm serious, now promise me you'll call."

"I promise, besides its kind of nice that I still have someone that actually cares. Now I've really got to go."

By the time the DCC returned to the conference room it was beginning to look more like the war room. Maps had hastily been put up there were drawings of the football stadium from a crowd control point of view.

Fresh refreshments were brought in and the DCC returned to the podium. "Gentlemen, I assume from what I see before me you have your plans. Do you have a central spokesperson who can brief me?"

All eyes went to Nick. "I suppose, sir that might be me. Besides, if I forget anything I'm sure someone will remind me."

He made his way to the front as Hardcastle took a cup of tea and sat down.

Nick started, "As we don't have an actual time we have started to call it **'H'** hour and we have set up a three point strategy: Before H Hour, at H Hour and afterwards."

"Depending upon when H Hour is exactly, we need to have eyes on all the keys players of both sides in advance. Also we recommend that all the stadium staff are rounded up and held incommunicado and secure prior to the operation. All normal staff positions will be filled by officers from the Armed Response Unit. Plus other ARU officers will be strategically placed under cover within the stadium well in advance of H Hour. I presume that the Stringers have their own contact inside the stadium staff and that we know who he or she is and can deal with them accordingly."

He was relieved to see the DCC smile and nod in response. "It's perfectly clear that neither side trusts the other. Both sides will suspect a trap and both sides will have lookouts posted around the area. We need to know who and where they are and neutralise them before they can raise the alarm. To be doubly sure, it would be nice if we could arrange a mobile phone blackout to prevent any premature warnings being given. To the same end we will not use standard police frequencies to coordinate this operation. It's fairly certain that the opposition will be scanning police radio traffic, so we will be creating a diversionary incident on the other side of town. It will take the form of a major road traffic accident involving a petrol tanker and a bus. We will be flooding the air with false messages giving the impression that all police and other emergency service activity will be concentrated on that area."

"All the main exits from the stadium open outwards so they can be easily blocked by a vehicle. Unmarked cars will be used to achieve this as soon as we know the lookouts have been silenced. At the same time road blocks will be set up at all roads leading to and from the stadium. Backup teams of uniform officers will be on hand, in case of a breakout, although it is our intention to contain the activity within the stadium itself."

"It is, however, anticipated that a great deal of firearms will be present on both sides and we may have to demonstrate our superior fire power before we can safely affect arrests. The police helicopter will be airborne but not in the immediate vicinity until called in."

As Nick stopped talking the room fell unnaturally silent while the DCC digested all that he had heard.

When he spoke it was to ask, "And you can achieve all this, phone blackouts and all?"

"Yes sir, all we need is H Hour and your blessing."

Hardcastle returned to the podium. "The meeting is set to take place with the main players in the centre of the field at 23: 30 tonight. You can assume that all other members will be close at hand. Start the count down and brief your men on a strictly need to know basis only. There is no need for anyone outside of this room to know what we know. I warn you now, the Stringers have eyes and ears everywhere, the slightest whiff of a trap and they will vaporise. Above all I want no heroics out there and no police casualties there will be a press blackout and I want no leaks. All… and I do mean all, mobile phones stay here… at base."

"Very well done gentlemen… there's nothing like a good crisis to concentrate the mind! Let's get this place tidied up before we go… leave no clues to our purpose tonight. Deploy your troops and be back here by twenty-two hundred at the latest, come in dribs and drabs… we will coordinate from here. Good luck and good hunting."

Slowly and without fuss the stadium was cleared of all normal staff, they were taken to a local hotel and after they handed over their mobile phones they were given a meal and made very comfortable.

Under the disguise of two football teams for a training session Nick moved the ARU officers and their equipment into place. He in turn found the central control room where he could control the flood lights and the public address system. Other officers took over the positions previously occupied by the ground and other staff members, so on the surface all looked normal.

Towards late evening, activity in the stadium wound down and the extra bodies drafted in for the purpose drifted away as the place shut down for the night. If anybody were watching, and they had to assume the place was under surveillance by at least one side but more probably both, then Nick and his team had made everything look as normal and boring as possible. Those still inside settled down for long silent vigil.

Outside in the nearby streets CCTV cameras, normally switched off on non match days, were active and manned. And it was not too long before shadowy figures could be seen lurking around. Closer looks revealed there were four lookouts, two black and two white. Surveillance on the opposing sides also revealed that each was watching the other.

At 22:43 hours police radio traffic indicated a major RTA at a roundabout on the far side of town, involving a petrol tanker and a coach load of old aged pensioners returning from a day out. Full emergency services were requested and all officers not attending other duties.

In the radio control room at police Head Quarters DCC Hardcastle was pacing the floor some distance from the other observers, and he seemed to be muttering to himself and nodding a lot. It was obvious he was in contact with someone but it was a secret he kept to himself. With a final and very definite nod of his head he came back to the main area with a smile on his face and announced; "It's on! They can't believe their luck that we are otherwise engaged and will be for some time to come. The Stringers are preparing to move out, and just in case there was any doubt on the subject they are tooled up for a war."

The deal was that all members from both sides would meet outside in the road by the club car park and player's entrance. They would all go in together as one group. As both sides approached the stadium, they were observed making contact with their own lookouts before proceeding further. Everybody appeared happy because minutes later the gangs moved towards the locked car park gates leaving the lookouts in place. Nick had arranged that, as soon as the mobile phone masts covering the area went down, the lookouts would be the first men arrested. That would signal the net to close.

It was quite a sizable crowd that stood facing one another in the near darkness, almost like fans of opposing teams on cup final day. One of the Stringer group broke free and walked towards the gates, seconds later the gates swung open and everybody trooped through. Hardcastle watched the CCTV monitor with a wry grin as Stringers man closed and locked the gates behind them.

There had been a strict radio silence all day, even on what they assumed was their own secure channel. Brief messages had been passed by a coded sequence of microphone trigger presses that gave only static as a noise. High in the grandstand Nick watched through a night vision scope, as the two teams came onto the pitch in front of him. He had been listening to Hardcastle's running commentary in his earpiece and a quick count of heads confirmed that no one had peeled off under the cover of darkness. He thought to himself, perhaps the Stringers are playing it straight, for once, maybe they have come to cut a deal.

Three loud static clicks in very quick succession told everyone listening, the phone system was down and the lookouts had been taken care of. Two minutes later, two quick clicks followed by another two clicks announced all gates and doorways secure.

There was a series of loud thumps as one by one the corner floodlights cracked into life, and the whole field was awash with light. An initial whistle from the public address system was followed by a booming voice:

"ARMED POLICE, GIVE YOUSELVES UP. I SAY AGAIN: ARMED POLICE, GIVE YOUSELVES UP.

PUT ALL WEAPONS ON THE GROUND AND THEN LIE FACE DOWN WITH YOUR ARMS AND LEGS SPREAD."

Initial shock was followed almost instantly by everybody on the field running in every direction. Nick was prepared for this as the sound of a rapidly firing machine gun echoed around the stadium.

"I REPEAT, YOU ARE COMPLETELY SURROUNDED, ARMED POLICE, GIVE YOUSELVES UP.

PUT ALL WEAPONS ON THE GROUND AND THEN LIE FACE DOWN WITH YOUR ARMS AND LEGS SPREAD."

The sudden burst of gunfire seemed to have the desired effect, at least on the Stringer side. But at least two Yardies reached for their weapons and fired at no one in particular. This time the sound that rang out was a single shot and one of the Yardie group fell to the ground motionless.

Once more Nick repeated his warning, as more and more people gave up and surrendered. The fact that they were in the middle of a floodlit football pitch faced with an opposition shrouded in total darkness. It did not stop the shouts of abuse as each gang accused the other of a sell out.

For added effect if they were looking at the giant TV screens at each end of the stadium they would have seen a small armoured car and a lot of armed soldiers moving in on their position.

The ARU officers broke cover and moved in to secure the entire area, retrieve and make safe a small arsenal of weapons. All the prisoners were searched for secreted weapons and ammunition, as well as their phones and any other evidence such as drugs. Only then were the doors unlocked and uniformed officers came in to take the prisoners away for detention and interrogation.

Back at police HQ Hardcastle was beside himself with joy, standing as he was at the very centre of a circle of congratulating other ranks. Leading the cheering was none other than the Chief Constable himself who said, "tell me again the final tally?"

Harcastle, chest pushed out, "Thirty-one arrested with only one fatality, one of the Yardies... unfortunate, but he gave us little choice... He was squirting off an Uzi machine gun... had to be taken out."

The Chief Constable replied, "Quite so, quite so, and speaking of squirting machinegun fire, I thought I heard gun fire as they started to scatter, and an armoured car and troops where the hell…?"

Hardcastle beamed at his boss…"Both Burton's idea, Sir. The machine gun burst was a tape recording, says he got the idea from some movie or other."

"And the troops?"

"Another bluff, I'm afraid. Old video tape, remember the contingency training we did after the 9/11 terrorist attacks in the USA, when we used the football stadium as a holding area and the Territorial Army as backup."

"Well damn good show, that's all I can say! Major success for a joint ops. Let's hope we can piece together enough evidence against them to put them away for years."

"Immigration and the drug boys will take the Yardies off our hands. They a series of coordinated raids going on right now on all their homes, our people are in support. We will handle the Stringers ourselves, been looking forward to it for years."

The Chief Constable was delighted with the night's effort…"Well all I can say is… a damn fine job, very well done! Give my sincere congratulations to Burton when he gets back, you tossed him in the deep end, and by God he did you proud."

Nick was far from resting on his laurels. Ceasing the golden opportunity that the DCC's major scheme had opened up, he called in both the day and night shift and started carrying out raids all over the Stringer Empire. If they were down, he for one wanted them to stay down and this was an opportunity not to be missed. He would argue the overtime bill later.

Chapter 7

The euphoria of the night before was over. Nick sat behind his desk; shirt collar undone, tie pulled down, face unshaven. He looked and was tired. It had been a hell of an operation and a tremendous success but the real work was only just getting started.

Already he was being harassed by lawyers representing the senior members of the Stringer clan. The Stringers were one of the richest families around and they could afford the best. Everything would have to be by the book. The fact that they were all caught bang to rights in a clandestine meeting with rival drug dealers and that the police had recovered enough weaponry to start a small war was beside the point. Proof and evidence was all that mattered and his team would be hard pushed for days to come.

Mary came in with large cups of real coffee. "I'm thinking of bringing my bed in here don't suppose we're going home any time soon."

"We need to reorganise ourselves, we can't let tiredness weaken us, not against these shysters or they'll eat us alive. It won't do for their clients to be resting in the cells while we work ourselves into the ground."

As he sat there sipping his coffee it suddenly dawned on him that, for one reason or another, he had not had a decent night's sleep in days. What about tonight? Would she come? After all, in all the excitement he had not remembered to call her. Unlike his earlier prediction, his recent nocturnal activities had gone on too long and been kept so quiet that they had failed to make the morning papers. Not so the TV. The story broke about 08:30 and the press office at HQ became inundated. Fortunately, his part had been missed and his station remained unscathed. Should he call her now, what would he say? He took the risk and dialled.

The phone rang twice before being answered. "I'm not speaking to you."

"I'm sorry. You don't know what it's been like down here…"

"I know there were bullets flying and that you were probably in the thick of it, and I've worried myself half to death wondering who got shot..."

"I thought they said on the news that it was one of the bad guys..."

"That was the eleven o'clock news, you sod, and nobody told the press anything. Just that during the night a lot of people were arrested and someone got shot."

"Are you coming down?" he asked.

"If I do, I'm not speaking to you, so tell me were you in the middle of all that?"

"Nowhere near it... I was miles away…"

"Liar! There's a train that gets into Kings Cross about half past six. I might be on it, if I've forgiven you that is." The line went dead before he could respond.

He decided that the best course of action would be to go home and shower, change his clothes and get something to eat. Before he went he reviewed what everyone was doing and reorganised them into shifts, sending home the ones he knew who had been on duty as long as he had.

It is amazing how long pure adrenalin will keep you going, but when you stop and allow the body and mind to relax you feel physically drained and mentally exhausted.

In the shower Nick pondered the long list of things he needed to do so the momentum of Hardcastle's surprise initiative would not run out of steam. He thought too of six thirty and the other task in hand. Was she really as mad at him as she sounded? Would he have to rebuild bridges once more before getting to the truth of Dan Davies's alternative activities? Either way he could not just jump in with both feet, demanding to know as soon as she got off the train. He thought, nice meal, bottle of wine back here for a nightcap and then perhaps…

Sod that! Once he reached perhaps, his mind took a completely different route and he would learn nothing new if he followed that line. No! He would just have to take his chances over dinner and then after that if there was a perhaps, then Dan Davies wouldn't get in the way.

Back in the office he was straight into the thick of once more. They brought in the Fraud Squad, the Drug Squad, the Inland Revenue and Customs as they launched an all out attack on every aspect of the Stringer Empire. He was determined that the overly large team of shysters that represented the Stringer family were going to earn their fat fees this day.

He left the office in full swing in plenty of time to reach London and the railway station. He didn't want to add being late to the list of misdemeanours against him. As it was, he didn't have to wait long. As he stood scanning the late evening commuters heading home, he saw the Cambridge train clatter to a halt. He watched people pour off it, a lot of young people heading for a night out in the big city, and then his heart gave a little jump as he caught the first glimpse of her. She hadn't found sight of him yet, and there was an anxious look to her expression as she glanced around. He moved towards her and all of a sudden she saw him and launched herself into his arms. As he held her tight he could feel moisture on his cheeks and knew she was crying.

"Hey! What's all this?"

She pushed herself away with a little nervous laugh. "I'm not sure I could ever marry a policeman, my nerves won't stand it."

"It's not as bad as all that, most of the stuff we deal with is routine and pretty boring really. We don't get shot at all that often and besides, it wasn't anywhere nearly as bad as the press and the media made out."

"But... someone did get shot?"

"Yes, one of the bad guys... Damn shame really, he was just a kid, seventeen, eighteen years old. I suppose he panicked when the floodlights went on and squirted off a few rounds at nobody in particular. An ARU officer responded with a single shot."

"And where were you, exactly, while all this was going on, may I ask?"

"Nowhere near the frontlines... I assure you... I was up in the control room above the grandstand switching the lights on, that's all. I didn't go onto the pitch until everybody was searched and handcuffed. Now how about an early dinner, I don't know about you but I could eat a horse, well a small one anyway."

"Fine, but I suppose you wouldn't consider a change in career, would you?"

The meal was almost over and they had talked about practically everything in the world except what Nick most wanted to hear. It was obvious to him that she wasn't going to broach the subject and so it was up to him. While they waited for coffee he stretched over and took her hands in his. "We still have some unfinished business of our own you know?"

She smiled weakly at him. "I know, but not here OK?"

"We could go back to my place if you like." "I'll come, only if you promise not to use thumb screws or any of your other fiendish tools."

She must have said it louder than she intended or her voice had carried just a little too far because the old couple on the next table gave them a very startled look indeed.

Once at his flat Nick made coffee and put some music on, anything to avoid the horrible silence that had descended over them since leaving the restaurant. It was his fault, he knew but he had to get to the truth one way or another and he was reluctant to wait any longer.

She was sitting on the settee with her legs pulled up under her as he gave her the coffee. A sudden impression of a naughty little girl waiting for daddy to come home came unbidden into his mind. Whatever she knew scared her, he was after all a policeman and she had no idea what he would do with the information once it was out in the open.

Sitting down in an armchair opposite where he could see her clearly he said, "So, tell me a story."

She took her time, sipping her coffee, fidgeting in her seat to get comfortable. "Where do you want me to start?"

"All I want to know is what made someone as straight and level headed as Dan Davies suddenly go out one morning and decide to commit murder. Did one of your experiments go wrong or what?"

"No! It was nothing like that, the university was not involved. We were as shocked as anyone else when we found out. You see, Dan left a letter behind for the professor."

"But you are involved surely you egged him on, what was it the professor called him, one of his star pupils? So you must have had some inkling."

"No… No we didn't! Honestly, we didn't, you must believe me. Yes Dan was a star pupil, in many ways. As far as we know he's the only one ever to have met another living person during an out of body experience. You know that the other person he saw was Colin Murray."

"Yes! So what? Dan saw the accident happen and he also knew the man was flat on his back, paralysed."

"But did you know that Dan had seen him again?"

Now that was something he didn't know. "You mean Dan was visiting him in hospital?"

"No, not like that... Dan was experimenting by himself, at home. He said he had been moving around the town watching, testing to see how far he could go, how quickly and how fast he could return. He had done it many times before, I admit we prefer that students do these things under supervision but once the technique is mastered we are powerless to stop them. It was during one of these solo trips that he saw Colin Murray again out of his body and floating above the town. Dan reckoned he was looking for something, or somebody."

"Did you know that Murray could do this?"

"Not until Dan told us, no, he must be self taught. We went to see him at the time of the accident of course, just as we went to see every patient who would see us. Colin Murray seemed indifferent to our approach. If he was aware of our presence he never showed it in any way. We tried follow-up visits but, according to the hospital staff, he was totally unresponsive to all attempts by them to improve his lot in life. His only attempt at communications was via a blink light. You know one blink for yes, two for no. Even that was given up when his answers were almost completely negative."

"Self taught you say, is that possible?"

"There's no logical reason why not. He may have seen something about astral projection or something like it on TV. It's been talked about often enough. The process itself is not that hard to master, I could teach you in a few minutes. Colin Murray had fifteen years to work it out."

Then Nick remembered something, something Mary Riley had told him. "After he was killed the nursing staff was actually relieved by his death. I dismissed it at the time but apparently they used to tell each other scary stories about lights going on and off, things falling off shelves and trolleys for no good reason. One nurse swears she was groped while in the room alone with him. They said he could slow his heart right down to set off some sort of alarm or something just to get attention. As I said at the time I had no idea what to think about it."

Jilly was not smiling. "My God... If he could interact with other people while out of his body, no wonder Dan was alarmed."

"Why should Dan know… and wouldn't he have told you lot? And by the way, what do you mean by interact with others?"

"Imagine what it would be like to influence things around you without actually touching them. You said he could switch lights on and off. Now imagine using the same power to reach out and touch someone and know that they could feel it. Think about it, My God, you could just float down to the railway station and push someone under a train. We've got to take this to the professor. Will you come with me?"

"Jill, I can't just drop everything, we're right in the middle of a major investigation. As important as this is and as much as I want to get to the bottom of why Dan did what he did, I can't just stop what I'm doing and leave. You said Dan wrote a letter, what did he say?"

"I don't know. It was addressed to the professor. He never showed it to us, he just said it was related to what we were seeing on the news and that we should be very careful in what we said and to whom."

"Perhaps by the weekend things will have settled down, I can come up to you, say Sunday… could the professor do lunch?"

"Do lunch? Try and stop him, for this he'd probably cook it and serve as well."

Nick sat dumfounded at her sudden mood change, she was almost euphoric.

She smiled at him and asked, "You really have no idea how big a deal this is… have you?" She was beaming through tears of absolute joy as she scrambled to her feet on her way to him. "My very own personal dumb cop…" and she threw herself into his lap wrapping her arms around his neck.

Delighted as he was at this dramatic change in her, he had to admit that she was right, he had no idea what was happening or why. "Would you settle down and explain why the hell you are so excited?"

"If I said Eureka, would that help?"

"I reek of what?"

"Not you reek...dummy... Eureka! All my working life I've been waiting for this moment, proof of the professor's theories. Lots of people have had out of body experiences, most of them don't want to repeat them, it's usually far too traumatic for them. But every now and then we came across someone like that lady you saw on the video, and Dan who actually enjoy the experience. Some people can master levitation or telekinesis while others use other psychic powers. But until now we have never found any one person who could master more than one talent. That is until Colin Murray."

"But my beautiful nutcase, he's dead or had you forgotten?"

A little deflated she went on, "But there are witnesses, the nurses we must interview the nurses!" She was bouncing on his lap.

"But I still don't understand why you think mentally groping a nurse is such a fantastic breakthrough."

"It's the fact that she felt his touch that's the breakthrough, not what he did with his power, dumb ass!"

"Just set it up for Sunday and maybe we can get to the truth of what's going on. Now I hate to be indelicate but I haven't been to bed in nearly three days so..."

"Sleep! How can you think about sleep at a moment like this..."

He put his arms around her and stood up. "Who said anything about sleep?"

Sunday was a long time coming, the work was just piling up in every direction. In spite of his careful plans his staff was working far too many hours and were getting tired and cranky. So he used the solicitor's dislike of weekend working to his advantage and made sure his extended staff took full advantage of the time off to relax a little.

He was in a thoughtful mood as he travelled the short train journey to Cambridge. If the professor was as exhilarated as Jilly had been, it might be difficult to slow him down and discuss Dan Davies at all. It would be up to him to keep them focused, or at least try.

Jill met him at the station with a big girlish hug. "The professor can hardly wait for you to arrive he has so many questions."

"But I don't know anything more than I told you, it's all hearsay anyway, young nurses over reacting to scary stories."

As they walked along hand in hand she replied, "We don't think so and if Dan was aware of any of it he didn't think so either."

Once out in the station yard they got into her car and drove off.

"Look, this is all well and fine and I'll go along so far, but at the end of the day all I want is to see that letter, the one that Dan wrote to the professor and hopefully get to the truth of why he murdered Colin Murray."

He could feel a sudden drop in temperature as the smile disappeared from her face, the little girl he had fallen in love with was once more the serious Doctor

Tindell. "Listen Nick, I hear what you say, but please can you try and be a little less than PC Plod for a few hours? We are talking about a man and his life's work here. A life where he has suffered ridicule at the hands of his peers, branded as an eccentric loony and known as that nutty professor. Yes, I agree some of his theories are a little extraordinary, that's why to have real proof for just one of those theories is so important. As you know he is not a well man, and no one knows how much longer he can work or actively contribute. Personally I won't let his theories die with him but I would like to see some official recognition for his work before it's too late for him, is that too much to ask?"

"I have no idea which side of the fence I am any more. A few weeks ago I would have been firmly in the Nut Squad camp, now I just don't know. It seems to me that he's way out there in the 'Beam me Up Scotty' world of travel. Don't get me wrong, I for one would love him to be right. Let's just say I respect what you're trying to do so let's see if we can reach some form of joint conclusions and take it from there, deal?"

"Deal!"

The car was not even at a complete stop before the front door of the house was flung open and the figure of professor Harman-Jones was in the door frame. Out of his wheelchair, which he insisted was only for state occasions he seemed to be managing with the aid of a stout walking stick. Nick was not sure why he was surprised, but once inside there was a Mrs. Harman-Jones as well. A woman as smart and elegant as her husband was dishevelled with his wild hair and beard as untamed as ever. It was Mrs. Harman-Jones who took immediate charge, leading her over-excited husband back inside to his armchair by an open fire as she welcomed Jilly and Nick to their home.

Formal introductions out of the way, glass of sherry in hand, Eleanor Harman-Jones declined Jilly's offer of help and retired to her kitchen as the professor wasted no more time launching himself into his quest.

"Well my boy, thank you for coming. You have no idea how important this is to me, the promise of proof at last."

Nick smiled at the old man's enthusiasm and didn't want to be the cause of any disappointment but this was a man of science after all and like him, supposedly a seeker of truth.

"I'm sorry professor, but you do realise that the man is dead, everything else is pure hearsay?"

"Yes, yes I understand all that," it was said with a high note of irritation, "but the testimony of the doctors and nurses alone will go along way. And, there are the actions of Dan Davies, don't you see?"

"No Sir, I'm afraid I don't. All I see is a normal rational human being suddenly and inexplicably taking another human life. That in my book is wrong Sir, and there can be no justification."

"Ah! Yes! Yes I see… I see, from a policeman's perspective it must seem totally wrong but what if there were no choice?"

Eleanor returned and ushered everyone to the dining room for lunch. "I know him of old," she said looking sternly at her husband, "he would live on tea and sandwiches from a tray on his lap, if I let him. And he would inflict the same on you two given half the chance."

No sooner were they seated comfortably enjoying a selection of hot and cold smoked fish with hot buttered toast when he returned to the attack. "So what do you think, my boy?"

"Well sir, it seems to me that we always have choices, there is always an alternative, or at least there always has been in my experience."

"You're quite right of course, but in my world there is a very high degree of scepticism from the world around me about what I am doing and what I hope to achieve."

He stopped speaking and seemed to go into a meditative state. Nick was going to say something but a quick glance at Jilly changed his mind. She gave her head a little shake and then with her eyes and a slight nod indicated that he should watch the professor and pay attention.

Before his eyes, the crystal salt seller rose off the table, wobbled a bit and then appeared to float towards the professor.

Eleanor grabbed the offending condiment with a tart, "No you don't," followed by, "tell me why it's always the salt? You know the doctor's orders!"

Jill smiled as the professor seemed to return to normal and looked sheepishly at his wife. "How well you know me my dear."

"Sorry my boy, just an old man's parlour tricks."

Nick was open mouthed, "How is that possible? Was that an illusion or something?"

"No illusion," replied Jilly, "the professor was giving you a firsthand demonstration of the power of his mind."

"You mean will power?"

The professor smiled indulgently, much as a parent would to a particularly dull child. "A little like that, yes, just showing off, I can of course lift and control heavier objects and once or twice I have achieved self levitation."

"Once after falling over on his silly face for not using his sticks," Eleanor added with a stern look in her husband's direction.

The Professor ignored her interruption. "Point is I have mastered telekinesis, and I can leave my body, at will, almost as well as Dan could. What I can not do is perform telekinesis while I am out of my physical body. I can control direction, speed and location but other than observe I can not do anything."

Nick's face was deadly serious, as he watched Jilly help Eleanor clear the first course dishes and replace them with dishes of steaming vegetables as the professor stood up and started to carve away at a giant piece of roasted beef.

"I hope you brought your appetite with you, I like my meat on the rare side, how about you?"

"Rare is fine with me sir," as a large slice of beef, crisp and black on the outside changing colour to pink and then almost red raw by the bone, filled one side of his plate.

"My God," remarked Jilly, "a good vet could have that thing on its feet in a week, how can you two eat it like that? I'll have mine from the top, if you don't mind."

There was an appreciative silence while all four tucked into what was, as far as Nick was concerned, the best meal he could remember eating in a very, very long time. He returned the conversation to the point where the professor had left it.

"You say you can not do anything but observe while you are out of your body, but surely that's a good thing, isn't it?"

"Think of the possibilities…you leave your body and float free… travel where you will…what if when you get where you're going you could somehow anchor yourself there and just simply awaken, journey over."

"As a life long sufferer of motion sickness I applaud your idea but I must say I find the whole idea frightening in the extreme. I am only now getting to grips with the thought of people floating about everywhere observing everything. Which I might add opens up the thought of terrible consequences in the hands of people like MI5 and the like. That's not to mention what criminals would do if they were to get hold of the skill, I shudder to think what might happen. Now you say it may be possible to float off and then do something when you get there?"

Nick continued; "Professor, I've seen your video's and heard you speak and I must say what little I understand scares me. Speaking as a policeman you must see the dangerous possibilities of what you and your colleagues are doing here? It's an unfortunate fact of life that practically every great discovery made by man has been used by other men as a weapon first. Now you say there is the possibility of remotely killing someone, completely undetected. How could we ever hope to police such a crime?"

The professor was stunned into silence his usual enthusiastic response was not there. Clearly he had never ever considered that there could be a negative side to his work. He looked shattered.

Main course finished, dessert was a relatively quiet affair while the professor and Jill absorbed his comments. In the meantime Nick took the opportunity to thank and congratulate Eleanor for a wonderful meal and he used the opportunity to talk of other subjects with her.

The look that Jill gave him was a little cold, when she spoke it was tinged with sadness and a hint of anger after all it wasn't just the professor's bubble he had just burst but hers too. "So in a nutshell what you saying is that we should stop what we're doing immediately and go and do something less frightening, is that it?"

Nick looked around the table. From Eleanor's look it was obvious that she had witnessed more than her fair share of earth shattering debates at her meal tables. He replied, "I'm not saying that at all, what I'm saying is that perhaps you should pay a little more attention to the fact that there is a potentially dangerous downside to your work. Maybe get an objective outside opinion now and again, just for balance."

"You mean someone like you?" Again there was coolness in her voice.

But before he could respond and possibly say something he would instantly regret the professor was back with them.

"Of course you're absolutely right..." he sniffed... never gave it much thought before now, but yes, I see now, the potential consequences..." and he was gone once more.

"Coffee in the lounge I think," Eleanor said, "and afterwards perhaps you two would like to walk off your lunch while I get him to take a nap, back in time for tea perhaps."

Either the lunch or the professor's change of heart had mellowed her as they walked she slipped her arm through his. She put her head against his arm. "If that's you taking it easy on somebody remind me never to piss you off."

He put his arm around her shoulder. "Sorry but I think it needed saying that's all. The more I listened to the two of you talking the more I realised that neither of you had considered the darker side of what you're doing."

"L-u-k-e! Come and join me on the dark side of the force," she said in a low growl of a voice.

"Are you saying I'm wrong?"

"No damn it, you're right and I think the professor agrees with you. Our meeting in the morning is going to be kind of interesting though, especially after he has slept on it,…if he sleeps at all that is."

They arrived back at the house by teatime, as instructed and the professor was already awake.

"Wondered where you two had got to, trouble with sex and romance tends to blunt the scientific mind."

With mock horror Eleanor snapped at him. "That's enough out of you on that subject, especially on a Sunday."

The professor just sniffed and with a wink to Jilly he added, "Quite a find you have here. Should we put him on the team?"

Sitting down by the fire Nick came straight out with it. "Professor, before he died Dan sent you a letter. Could I read it, if it's not too personal?"

With a grin the professor replied, "Surprised you didn't ask before, perhaps in light of our lunchtime conversation I should read it again as well."

He passed the document over to Nick.

At the same time Nick reached into his jacket pocket and pulled out some folded sheets of paper. "Instead

Sir, perhaps you wouldn't mind casting your eyes over these reports." He passed the professor the file that he had received anonymously through the post.

As the professor changed spectacles Nick opened the letter, the last one Dan ever wrote. It was dated two days before he died.

Dear Professor,

By the time you read this certain events that I have set in motion will be complete and I will have moved on.

If I have any regrets it is that I was unable to confide in you certain facts that came to me in my official capacity as a police officer. However, let it be sufficient for me to say that I carried out extensive enquiries using all of my <u>powers</u> and came to a satisfactory conclusion that I had found the correct perpetrator of the crimes in question.

I honestly believe that without my direct intervention this man will continue his activities until at least two maybe three other people die. There is absolutely no way I can effect a satisfactory conclusion using my police powers people would think I was off my head. When you see what I have done you too may agree with them.

I take full responsibility for my actions and it is my intention to protect all the people I care for and love by taking the secret of my action to the grave.

If for whatever reason I inadvertently damage your work them I can only offer my most sincere apologies and beg for your forgiveness that was never my intent.

Yours in haste,
Dan Davies.

Nick read the letter twice more, folded it up and looked over to where Jilly had moved over and was now sitting on the arm of the professor's chair, reading the reports he had brought with him. Without a word he handed the letter back to the professor who passed it to Jill. At that moment in time he could have sold them the moon on a string. The mood in the room was sombre.

Jilly spoke first. 'Why didn't you show me these earlier?'

Nick replied, "For what purpose? At the time they had no significance for me. Police files are full of the weird and the unexplained. It's like the nurse's story, spooky but from an evidence point of view, useless."

The professor removed his reading glasses and spoke in a gentle voice, "Me too, when I received the letter I couldn't grasp the true significance of it at all. Even when I read in the newspapers what had happened I still couldn't accept it for what it was. Now," and he held up the reports in emphasis, "I assume that this is what Dan was referring to in his letter?"

'That is my conclusion too, yes Sir."

"Well my boy, you were right to be scared by what you see us do. As for me, blundering old fool that I am, it seems I am also an accomplice to murder."

Jill dropped to her knees by his side and took his hand in hers. Eleanor rose from the settee and came to his side defensively.

He continued, "I will of course tender my immediate resignation in the morning and make myself available to you if that's alright with you, young man?"

Nick's jaw dropped. "Sir! I didn't come here to arrest you, or even to accuse you of anything. Why would you resign your post?"

"I would have thought that should be obvious to you, it most certainly is to me. I am the teacher, Daniel Davies was my pupil. I taught him how to use the power of his mind and it drove him to take the life of an innocent man. Who else is more responsible?"

Jill let out an anguished "No!" She looked to Nick to say something, her eyes filling with tears pleaded silently with him; Do something! Say Something!

"Sir, if I may. I don't wish to offend you in your own house especially after such a splendid lunch but you're talking complete nonsense. I'm the detective here, and we are both following a trail of clues. True, Dan was your student but Colin Murray most certainly was not. No one had any knowledge whatsoever that he had taught himself to use his mind in such a way. It was only on the hearsay of some nurses that I even became aware of it."

"On one of his trips Dan saw Murray out and about, so what? Perhaps he should have brought it to your attention, you or Jill but he didn't. He said Murray looked as if he was searching for something. What if that was searching for someone… like the people who put him where he was?"

"Think about it, these two reports; a man falls from on high in front of a train. Trouble is there wasn't anywhere on high to fall from. Question: could someone with the power of Colin Murray pick a person up and drop him from a great height? For me it is possible that the man… what was his name, William Smith… he could have been the getaway driver. He's the right age, has a criminal record involving cars, he lived all his life locally to the robbery scene and knew the area well. At the time of the actual robbery the getaway driver was never seen by any of the witnesses to the jewellery store robbery but Colin Murray might have seen him as he ran him over. It's circumstantial but it's possible."

"And the woman, Sue Ann Mackenzie, she's an actress, not a very good one by all accounts but I checked up on her and she was at least in the country at the time of the robbery. Even before the robbers entered the shop and damaged the cameras the CCTV footage of the customers, the old woman in the wheelchair, was so poor it could have been anyone. Perhaps even a young woman in stage makeup. As to how someone like Murray could permanently transform her into the old woman she portrayed on the occasion of that report is something maybe only the two of you can work out."

"For Dan's part, let's assume he was right in his conclusions, for all we know he may have witnessed Colin Murray committing the crimes. Let's face it in the police World... who was he going to tell? Who in their right mind would believe him? From what I've seen even by the standards of your own experiments Murray... if it was him, was way beyond your level. Dan couldn't just walk into the hospital and put Murray under arrest, he would have been laughed out of the force. Dan Davies was a logical man. He would have thought it all through, until he reached his solution. Our files on the original robbery are still open no one was ever caught or even suspected. The original conclusion that it was an out of town armed robbery by two men that went wrong is itself flawed."

"They supposedly took the old lady and her chauffeur hostage, they were bundled into the backseat of the Jaguar by one of the masked men. Someone else drove the car... that was supposedly her car. What happened to the original getaway vehicle, there should have been one? No cars were reported abandoned at the scene. No ransom note was ever received for the kidnap victims. Nobody matching their description was ever reported missing and no bodies were ever found. Conclusion, they were all in on it from the start, five people in all. That's what Dan was saying... one dead, one transformed, three to go. If he was right, and who can say either way, then eliminating Murray in the way he did was, for him, the best and only solution."

Concentrating hard and hanging on Nick's every word the professor said, "Just supposing your hypothesis is correct, and mind you I'm not saying that it is, surely I'm still partly to blame?"

Nick looked at the ladies and the concern etched on their faces and smiled at them all. "Can't see it myself, it doesn't fit the facts and there is no evidence linking you to any of what took place ..."

Jill jumped up off the floor and flung her arms around him saying to the room in general, "You'll have to excuse him... He does this all the time he sounds like somebody off crime watch."

Sounding muffled, he carried on, "If I may be allowed to finish, as you so rightly pointed out your research is confidential, if this story was to leak out the media would have a field day and your work would be destroyed. You mustn't resign, or even give up, as far as I can see your work is more important now than ever. Suppose for one minute that Colin Murray is not the only one out there with these powers. You have to take your research to its conclusion. You must find out if these things are truly possible and then find ways of containing them or at the very least ways of detecting them. The consequences of not doing so are too horrific to contemplate."

It was the professor who was first to comprehend Nick's words. "My boy, my boy, in the space of one afternoon you have taken my work apart and put it back together in the way it should be. It was passionately argued, if only some of my so called colleagues could have been here today….yes indeed." And it seemed as if he just drifted off into space.

"Time to go, I think," Jill remarked and Eleanor escorted them to the door and then to the car.

Eleanor gave Jill a big hug and kissed her on the cheek whispering in her ear, "I think you should try and hang on to this one, don't you?"

Jill smiled as she gave her cheek a kiss. Eleanor crossed to Nick and took his hand.

"I'm not exactly sure if you are friend or foe, I was hoping to talk that old bugger in there into retiring but after today…"

Nick smiled and shook her hand warmly. "Friend I hope, I would hate to think that I may never eat so well again. Thank you it was a truly marvelous meal and I'm sorry if I messed up your retirement plans."

Back in the car once more Jill asked, "So, where to now?"

"In what respect?"

"I don't believe you! You've just spent the last few hours turning my world upside down, giving it a bloody good shake and then you ask in that infuriating policeman's voice, in what respect," she mimicked him.

"Ah! I thought you meant your place or mine."

"In your dreams mister! We need to get a few things straight first."

"Such as?"

"Such as?" She mimicked. "This afternoon for a start, for a minute back there I thought you were going to destroy that man and everything he'd worked for all his life. You certainly rocked him pretty hard. And what about me, it's my world too you know?"

"I'm sorry you feel that way, that was not my intent, but if my dumb theory is even half right you must see the potential that lurks within the experiments you are conducting?"

"It's not that dumb a theory," she whispered with a little shiver. "And you've started me thinking that I may not be up to the job any more. It's just too sinister for me to think that I would be helping to develop some sort of super weapon. That's not me I want to use science to help the world not make it a worse place."

Nick responded, "Was Einstein evil, do you think if he could have foreseen Hiroshima and Nagasaki that he would have told the world that E equals MC 2 squared or whatever he said? You can't dis-invent something just because you disagree with what people find to do with your discovery. My God Jill… you should take a look at the world through my eyes. Practically everything ever invented by nature or man can… and probably has been used as a weapon of some sort to hurt, maim or kill people. Someone has to stand up and protect the little people why not you whose better qualified?"

She pulled into the station car park and stopped. Undoing her seatbelt she got as close to him as the front seats of her car would allow and took his hand and for the second time that day he saw tears in her eyes.

"I can't, I won't be party to research that creates people who would use the powers to kill and destroy. It's just wrong and I won't do it."

"So you'll just leave it to the professor… is that your solution? At least he can see the danger. Do you honestly believe that just because you drop out and pretend it doesn't exist that others will do the same? Do you think that the Americans, the Russians or God forbid some lunatic terrorist organisation isn't looking into and funding similar research? Don't you think it would be nice for our own country to have an edge or some kind of deterrent?"

"Of course I do, it's just…"

"I'm sorry Jill… I'm sorry if I rocked your comfy little boat. But if you are going to be part of my world you are going to have to wake up to the fact that the world is not a nice place. It's full of not very nice people who would probably kidnap and torture you for what you know already. We need…damn it… I need a way to keep you safe. And there's something else you'd better understand about me before we go much further forward, in my job, in certain circumstances I may not be the nice lovable person you think I am."

"I've seen a little of that Nick Burton, you try to keep him well hidden but he peeks out every now and then but I think he's only aimed at the bad guys, isn't he?"

He smiled at the scared little girl before him. How sheltered her protected world of academia had been until he had stomped through it with his policeman's boots. "I sometimes wake up in a cold sweat worrying that one day I may become as bad as they are."

"Nah! Not my Sir Galahad!" Now she was smiling but her eyes were puffy from the recent tears.

"Does that mean you'll do it?"

"Let me talk to the professor in the morning, I doubt he will sleep much tonight either. It will mean a total rethink of our department and the experiments and all."

"Not to mention the secrecy. Remember you're looking for a way to detect the activities of others not just performing them."

She pulled him towards her and kissed him with all the passion the confined space would allow. "Go home and give a girl time to think."

"Can't I stay and help?"

She laughed, "Some help you'd be. I want to take a long soak in the bath and let my mind roam. If you were there I don't think it would be my mind that would be roaming, do you?"

"Perhaps not, still, I have an hour or so I could scrub your back or something."

"Down boy… There will be plenty of time for all that later… but seriously, tonight I need to be alone, do you understand?"

He kissed her again, reluctant to let her go. "Yes damn it, of course I understand but I already hate the practical side of my nature."

Then with an impish grin she said, "Perhaps you'd better go before I start to hate that side of you too."

One final kiss and he was out in the cool evening air watching the tail lights of her car disappear into the passing traffic and was gone.

Chapter 8

Monday mornings were always a challenge, motivating the troops to go forth and do battle once more. Learning what horrors the local representatives of mankind had managed to inflict upon one another and wondering what, if anything, was expected from him and his over stretched group.

An official looking buff envelope caught his attention, sitting as it did on the top of the large pile of mail and other documents in his In Tray. He might have ignored it until later if it had not been for the fact that his name and rank was the only thing on the envelope and it was hand written. He tore it open and pulled out the letter from within. He recognised immediately the official police force letterhead but instead of some type written missive there was a short hand written note. He read it twice with a slight frown on his face it was an invitation to join the DCC for a drink after work.

The time was set for eight o'clock and the hotel chosen was not one of their usual police haunts. He was at once both intrigued and annoyed. It intrigued him because in all his years of service he had never once had such an invitation. It was a kind of honour, he supposed, certainly not something you could ignore, or send a polite note back saying, thanks but no thanks. Annoyed because after yesterdays activities he wanted to talk to Jill, possibly on the phone, but he really wanted to jump on a train and go. He smiled at the thought, how for the love of this woman he was spending more time travelling than he had done in years. How he was willing to suffer the discomfort of motion sickness just to be in her company for a few short hours. However, he recognised that at least for tonight he would have to settle for the phone call.

Then he wondered what Hardcastle really wanted. Couldn't be official police business or he would simply summon him to HQ. Nor could it be any kind of celebration, if it was why choose that hotel, it was a bit seedy if he was remembering the right place. Then with a sigh he resigned himself to wait and see trying to second guess Deputy Chief Constables was never a good idea.

He was in the bar of the hotel a good fifteen minutes early. His memory of the place had been correct; the owners were old and should have cut their losses and retired years ago. The place was musty and reeked of dust and decay. What customers there were seemed as old and as disinterested as the staff. He ordered an orange juice and lemonade in a tall glass with lots of ice.

"No ice," was the surly reply.

"Then I'll just have the orange juice."

"Brave man," the gruff voice of DCC Hardcastle spoke in his ear. "Best to drink neat spirits in this place, disinfects the glass if nothing else."

Nick looked at the poor selection of whisky behind the bar and ordered a double of what looked like the newest bottle, probably the landlords favourite, and handed it to the DCC.

"Thank you me boy," Hardcastle said with gusto, "Let's sit over there in the corner away from the crowd."

Nick looked around the bar, besides the barman and the two of them there were only two others in the whole room, still he did as he was told.

"Look, sorry to drag you away from your social life…"

"And what social life would that be, sir?"

From the look he got for his troubles Nick could have bitten his tongue out. It was the kind of look you get that says you don't get to be a DCC by being a dumb Prat.

"Sorry sir, you were saying."

"These past few weeks have been tough, especially upon you, death of a pal and all that, sudden promotion extra work and then this thing with the Stringers bit of a strain what?"

"We're coping sir, the extra help you managed to beg or borrow have been a great help. Plus the Drug, Customs and Immigration people are all taking their fair share of the work load."

Hardcastle tried to grab the attention of the man behind the bar who was doing his utmost to ignore him. "EXCUSE ME," Hardcastle shouted at the man and got the attention of the entire room. As surly as he was even the barman could not ignore the summons. Drinks refreshed, he continued:

"We're still looking to get a replacement for Dan, has to come from outside the division, of course, and bound to take time. Listen Burton, I've never been one for beating around the bush so I'll come straight to the point Superintendent Hodges handed in his final report of his investigation into the murder of Colin Murray by DCS Davies and to be quite frank it's a complete waste of paper, utter balderdash."

"Surely you're not surprised, sir. What exactly did you think he'd find out?"

"Damn it man, it wasn't his job to find out anything, it was his bloody job to come up with something to satisfy the press Johnnies, some sort of plausible story as to why Dan did it in the first place."

"With all due respect sir, that was a pretty tall order. Why not let the official record show that he committed a terrible crime while the balance of his mind was unstable. Call it severe depression following the death of his wife then he committed suicide for the same reason. The press may not be happy with that as an explanation but least said soonest mended."

"Why do you say that? You know more than you're letting on, aren't you? Out with it lad, damn it all Burton I know you've been poking around, doing it with my unofficial blessing as well you know, main point of coming to this sink hole was to find out how it's going."

In spite of the near empty room Nick lent forward and lowered his voice. "Sir, I don't know what to tell you. The only thing I've got is a half-cocked theory that would be unbelievable as a TV programme. It's certainly not the sort of thing we could ever release to the media, or anybody else for that matter, as a plausible explanation for anything."

Hardcastle, took a hard pull on his whisky. "Come on boy, out with it, I like a good yarn."

Nick took a deep breath…"Are you familiar with a man called professor Harman-Jones at all?"

"The nutty professor… sure… Great pal of Dan's, as I recall… Did quite a good magic turn at parties, quite amused the ladies by floating things off the table and that sort of thing, that the chap you mean?"

Nick was not buying this dumb old codger routine, it was a great wheeze of the DCC's to play the grand old retired military gent long past his sell by date. Full of 'what ho!' And 'don't you know'… it was a good act, fooled a lot of people but the secret was to look at the eyes. This was no old duffer,...the old bugger was a sharp as a tack and Nick knew it.

"That's him sir, well it seems that his party piece may not be a magic act after all. It turns out that the good professor runs a sort of Psychology department in Cambridge. They conduct studies into the subdivisions of the human mind, seeking out conscious and unconscious mental powers. He's also well versed in the arts of telekinesis and levitation and yes he can and does perform examples of both."

"By Jove, you're serious aren't you?"

"Yes sir, I am. The professor's department has made extensive studies into what they call 'out of body' or 'near death' experiences. That's where there is evidence that someone has apparently left their body and looked down upon themselves while floating up near the ceiling."

"I've read something of the sort in the Sunday papers, stuff and nonsense if you ask me, bright lights and angels that sort of rot... they should take more water with it in my opinion."

Again, the eyes betrayed him. Nick was watching him closely over the rim of his glass as he took a sip of his warm orange juice. The words were all bluff and bluster...behind the performance he was giving Nick his full and undivided attention.

"Trouble is, sir, that there are just too many credible accounts given to the professor and his people for them to dismiss it as casually as you or I would. For example were you aware that Dan was a pupil of the professor?"

"What do you mean a pupil, in the past you mean?"

"No sir, right up to the time of his death Dan Davies was not only a friend but also a student of professor

Harman-Jones. Dan had had an out of body experience himself, fifteen years ago when he got himself shot during the armed robbery of that big jewellery shop in the High Street."

"Did Dan himself tell you all this?"

"I suppose he did, in a way, he left a video tape explaining a few things, of course not what he did or why… but he did explain his experience. And at the time he gave such details that no one on the ground at the scene could possibly have seen. During the experience he witnessed the hit and run accident that put Colin Murray in hospital. He described it in far greater detail than is in any of the files, I've read them."

"Well I'll be damned! He never said a word about any of it to me."

"Not to anyone, outside Cambridge that is, pity really because if he had got you to believe him his eye witness account would have been a great help to the enquiry at the time. After it hit Colin Murray he saw the car speed away up the valley and then turn cross country to where the thieves obviously had another car or cars stashed. That shows good local knowledge, they abandoned the Jaguar and went on their merry way, all five of them."

"Wait a minute, I remember that case there were only two armed robbers that day, where the hell do you get five?"

"They were all in it, the old woman, assuming that she was old at all, her chauffeur and the unseen getaway driver, who drove them away in her Jaguar. That was the mistake that put me on to them. If it had been only the two robbers and a getaway man there should have been a getaway car abandoned outside the jewellers and there wasn't, they took the Jag. Why would the getaway driver suddenly change cars, and of course...surely it would have been locked? It doesn't make sense unless they were all in on it."

"Well I'll be... and you say Dan saw all this and put it together?"

"Not exactly Sir, Dan saw it yes, and explained it like a witness but it's only my theory as to what took place."

"Makes sense, so far, but it still doesn't explain why fifteen years after the fact Dan pops over to the local hospital and bumps off this Murray chap. I mean, dash it all, Murray wasn't part of the gang... was he?"

"No sir he wasn't. He was as much a victim of the gang as Dan was. But just like Dan, Murray had an out of body experience. Dan saw him..."

"Hold on a jiff, what do you mean Dan saw him?"

"Exactly that, while Dan was out of his body watching the getaway car make its escape, he witnessed the hit and run on Murray, who as a result also had an out of body experience. Dan was witness to it. They were both floating above the scene of the accident together. They never talked and Murray never acknowledged the fact that he could see Dan or was even aware of his presence but Dan saw him. And not just once, it happened again in the hospital where they were both taken. It's all in Dan's tapes."

"Tapes, why am I only now hearing about these bloody tapes? Where the hell did they come from?"

"Truth is sir, I'm not entirely sure. I seem to have my own personal Mr. X who has been spoon feeding me the odd tit bit of information. One of the tapes was made by Dan with the help of his pals at Cambridge. I think it was Dan's attempt to satisfy me and get me to accept the official verdict... that... and of course the professor and his staff, they were just too helpful too keen to convince me that they were not involved. But the first tape and the police reports, they came from Mr. or Ms. X."

"Police reports… Mr X you're making my head hurt, I need another of these," he drained his glass and raised his hand in the direction of the bar. Almost at once the barman nodded and brought more drinks.

Once the barman scuttled away Nick continued, "The reports were two recent unsolved cases involving mysterious and inexplicable circumstances. I can show them to you later, needless to say I didn't bring them with me. At first they only served to add to my confusion. Personally I couldn't see any link with anything. Yet I got the distinct feeling that somebody was trying to tell me something but I was too stupid to see what."

"DC Riley and I visited the Murray family to pay our respects and find out how they felt about the whole situation. To my amazement it was relief… well at least as far as the father was concerned it was, as if Dan had done him a favour. Following up a couple of casual remarks Riley visited the hospital and interviewed the nurses that had attended Murray and she got the same result. Relief! It was as if everyone was glad he was dead. The nurses told Riley stories of lights going on and off by themselves, the TV changing channels without anybody anywhere near it. Doors becoming jammed locking people in the room with him in the dark, spooky stuff like that."

Hardcastle sat mesmerised, just sipping his whisky as he listened to Nick's tale unfold.

Nick went on, "Then as I said, I'd had the VIP treatment at Cambridge, I'd seen their video taped experiments and they confessed that Dan was a star pupil of theirs and still the penny failed to drop. I had lunch with the professor just yesterday and made a discovery… apparently he can levitate his body, although I haven't seen him do it yet, but like you I have seen his party tricks. He reckons that he can lift quite heavy things but just for a short time."

"Then all of a sudden it hit me, just suppose… if the professor could, just with the power of his mind pull off his party tricks as you call them, what else could you achieve with mental power alone? Suppose it could be self taught, what might you achieve if you had fifteen years alone and inactive to work it out?"

"With the professor's guidance Dan could leave his body at will, just float away and observe. Apparently they were experimenting with distance trying to see how far he could go and how quickly he could return. The professor has a dream that one day this is how we will all travel."

Hardcastle snorted in disbelief. "You're not serious?"

"It's a little far fetched, I admit, but the leaving of the body at will is possible and they have proof of it on tape and under strict laboratory conditions. Christ, they even offered to teach me how to do it, it's that simple."

The DCC looked confused, "Where the hell are you going with this, you're beginning to lose me a little?"

"I'm sorry sir, I'm wandering a bit. I honestly believe that Dan was experimenting with his mind travels in his own time and away from the control of his minders in Cambridge. I think, and here I have absolutely no proof whatsoever, that on one of these trips he saw Murray again, also away from his body. I think Murray with fifteen years of bitterness and built up hatred inside of him was looking for revenge against those who put him where he was. He was seeking them out… and was dealing with them in the only way he could."

"You mean the two unsolved cases involving mysterious circumstances?"

"Yes Sir, I do and what's more I believe Dan thought so too, trouble was what could he do about it? Who could he tell? Would they believe him?"

"You're right of course… come to me with a cock and bull story like I've just heard and I would have laughed in his face… sent for the men in white coats… off his chump and no mistake… what?"

"Yes Sir… However I believe that's precisely what he did. He did come to you with the story. I've no idea how but he convinced you that he was right and that his solution was the only one possible."

Hardcastle's steely eyes bore right through him. "Dan always said you were a clever bugger. You were the weak link all along, he knew that too. He knew that you'd never accept the situation as it appeared on the surface. He said that you would make a bloody nuisance of yourself trying to get to the truth. So we made it easy for you to find the truth by yourself. Now you know."

"You knew everything all along, you're the one whose been playing me like a fish on a hook, it's you…you're Mr. X?"

Hardcastle sat back from the edge of his seat he first raised and then drained his glass. "You've put the pieces together quite nicely, if you don't mind me saying so. You're wrong on a couple of small points though… I didn't quite know everything, certainly not as well as I do now. You've done your usual bang up job... you are a damn fine detective I'll give you that. Secondly... I wasn't convinced with Dan's story, it just sounded too far fetched to me but I trusted his judgement and in the end short of having him committed there was little I could do to stop it happening. After all is said and done he could pick his moment."

"Question is now that you know what do you intend to do with the knowledge?"

"We're right back to square one, aren't we sir? Who in their right mind would believe me? Of course I'm sure the press could have some fun with the story but that would destroy the reputation of Dan Davies and worse his daughter. I think she'd be happier with the suicide theory following the death of his wife and her mother. As far as the professor and his staff are concerned, in my opinion his work must continue. After all... if I'm right and Murray managed to kill someone using only the power of his mind he is hardly likely to be unique in the world."

Hardcastle seemed satisfied. "One more for the road, then I'm off, busy day tomorrow, first of the real court cases involving the Stringers, should get them put away for years. My God lad Dan would have been proud of you for your efforts."

"It was really your show sir, me and mine only handled the logistics. Canny bit of luck on your part though, getting someone that deep under cover within the Stringer organisation. Must have taken months, hell of a risk, if the Stringers had found out we would have been looking for all the pieces for years."

Hardcastle sat there his face set like stone. "A risk worth the taking, wouldn't you say? That family has been a thorn in our side for generations we're well rid of them."

"Oh I quite agree there, but trouble is sir, their demise leaves a bit of a vacuum, and you know nature and crime hates a vacuum. How do we know we haven't just cleared the pitch for some other organisation to move in?"

"No doubt about it… we have… but hopefully next time we'll be ready, get 'em before they get their feet under the table. By the way…There's a rumour doing the rounds that as a result of the success the Chief Constable is setting up a new intelligence task force. You'll be heading it just as soon as we sort out replacements for you and Dan."

"Intelligence… Me? Are you sure sir, I mean… it's a great honour to be asked but…"

"Honour be buggered, it's you or nobody, our main man won't work with anybody else, by God lad, don't you see, this is the opportunity of a lifetime."

"Our main man, we have a mole? Am I permitted to know who it is?"

A soft gentle voice behind said, "I think that would be me."

In that split second of immediate recognition Nick spun around so fast his vision reeled and a wave of nausea overtook him. "You! But how in hells name…?"

There, now standing at his side stood the smiling figure of Dan Davies as large as life. He was slightly less dapper in his appearance, probably for obvious reasons and he was badly in need of a shave as if he was in the early stages of growing a beard. He offered his hand. "Hello Nick, I knew you'd never let it rest, you were bound to work it out in the end and I needed to know what you might do about it."

As Dan sat in a seat between Hardcastle and himself Nick found he had momentarily lost the power of cohesive thought as well as the ability to reason and talk. In the silence Hardcastle excused himself. "Got to go but I'm sure you two have some catching up to do… what? Besides I already know this bit of the story." And with a final 'Toddle Pip!' he was gone.

Nick just stared across the grimy table at the man he once called friend still speechless. He didn't know whether to rave at the man or congratulate him for being only the second man in history to rise from the dead. The only thing that came from his lips was a very croaky 'Why?'

Dan pulled himself forward in his chair and when he spoke it was in a quiet voice that even Nick had to strain to hear.

"I'm sorry for everything I've put you through but trust me it was the only way for me to achieve everything that needed doing without over complicating everything."

"Complicating everything! They carried your dead body from the police cells and put you in the morgue. We buried you for Christ's sake."

"As I said, trust me, I wasn't dead when they took me away, I merely slowed my heart down to a point that even an expert might be fooled. In this case an over worked police doctor with a drink problem it was risky but well calculated."

"What about the post mortem? I read the bloody report."

"Sorry about that… can't have a funeral without one, suspicious circumstances and all that. As you can imagine I scared the living daylights out of the pathologist when I sat upright still in the body bag. Known him for years, swore him to secrecy once I explained what was going on, told him it was all part of a police sting operation."

"So who the hell did we bury?"

"No one, just so much dead meat from the abattoir, smelled right if anybody got too close… pathologist chap took care of that as well."

"But what about Jenny…?"

"Ah! Now there I must ask you to swear to me that I stay dead. I will, like everybody else die one day and I'm not going to put her through all that again."

"But…"

"No buts Nick, I mean it, I'm dead to everyone who ever knew me save you and Hardcastle. Swear it now or I'll just up and disappear on you. No one would ever believe you and you've no proof."

"But why?"

"Let's just say I've burnt all the bridges behind me, and I have no regrets. Besides if I was to miraculously return to life that really would be big news, and what would it serve? And don't forget if I were still alive I would have to stand trial for murder."

"I'd forgotten about that, was that really necessary? I can't believe you went to Hardcastle and not me. I thought we were friends for God's sake."

"I trust we still are, but to answer all your questions, yes it was necessary. You have no idea how powerful Murray had become. I toyed with the idea of confiding in the professor but in the end decided against it. He would have wanted Murray transferred to him to study him or some such thing. I couldn't accept that, I knew the professor was no match for Murray and the bastard was getting stronger by the day. It was hard for me to keep track of him… but I could only observe. He could touch things, manipulate them. If I was to stop him it had to be in the physical world."

"As to why I didn't confide in you ask yourself this, if anyone came to you and said Nick old chap I'm just going to pop out and kill someone you won't mention it to anyone will you? You're a policeman for Christ's sake! Friend or no friend, you would have tried to talk me out of it or even stop me. I couldn't take the risk, was I wrong?"

Nick sighed a big sigh. "No… not really."

"Don't you see? If you hadn't gone through your whole investigation process you wouldn't believe me now. This way you at least accept that what Murray was doing and what I did to put an end to it is at least feasible. And, of course all of that aside you got to meet the very lovely Jilly which you wouldn't have done without my help. So, do I have your word?"

Nick smiled and stretched his hand over the table. "You have my word but not yet my forgiveness if that's OK?"

"I'll settle for that for the time being."

"Let me get something else straight, it was you inside the Stringers lair all this time feeding everything back to Hardcastle?"

Dan smiled… "Think about it, when you started to interrogate the various gang members and letting certain facts slip, the way you did. You turned them against one another. You were telling them things that only the highest family members knew. No ordinary informant or undercover agent could get that deep. This way the edge is in favour of the good guys."

Nick didn't return Dan's smile, "like I explained to the professor and Jilly the whole concept scares me rigid but it's a tool we can use. But you must promise me one thing, no more direct action, deal?"

"Deal! Now when the hell are you going to get that bloody ulcer of yours fixed so we can have a decent drink together? You know of course, you're the only pal I have in the whole wide world."

Two days later the local newspaper front page had a picture of Chief Superintendent Daniel Davies in full police uniform and a paragraph that read:

Police today released the official verdict following a lengthy enquiry into the sudden death of Chief Superintendent Daniel Davies. The report concluded that CS Davies was suffering from severe mental depression following the death of his wife and that he had committed suicide. CS Davies was a dedicated police officer who served his community for many years. He will be sorely missed.

The incident and connection with Collin Murray was not even mentioned.

Printed in the United Kingdom
by Lightning Source UK Ltd.
127609UK00001B/7-54/P